More Aster(ix) Anthologies

The Tarot Issue
December 2022

Mothers Unearthed
September 2022

Winter Fiction
December 2021

Best of Hot Metal Bridge
April 2021

The Ferrante Project
October 2020

The Poetry Issue
Winter 2020

Inheritance
Summer 2019

(Un)bound [double issue]
Winter 2018/2019

Edges - Fall 2018

Dirty Laundry - Fall 2017

Kitchen Table Translation - Summer 2017

and more!

available for order wherever books are sold

and don't forget to visit
asterixjournal.com
for more content and information

Aster(ix) Journal
www.asterixjournal.com

Editor-in-Chief/Founder
Angie Cruz

Publisher/Founder
Adriana E. Ramírez

Managing Editor
Amanda Tien

Contributing Editors for
The 10th Anniversary Issues
Laura Kenney
Sangi Lama
Sandra Lee
Paola Liendo
Avery Robinson
Kandala Singh
Megan E. Valley
Kira Witkin

Aster(ix) Contributing Editors
Rosa Alcalá, Arielle Greenberg, Yona Harvey, Daisy Hernández, J. A. Howard, Sheila Maldonado, Dawn Lundy Martin, Oindrila Mukherjee, Idra Novey, Emily Raboteau, Nelly Rosario, Zohra Saed, Sun Yung Shin, Jenelle Troxell, Chika Unigwe, Marta Lucía Vargas, Autumn Womack, Elleni Centime Zeleke

Advisory Editors
Ari Ariel, Armando Garcia, Amy Sara Carroll, Norma Cantú, Xochi Candalaria, Jennifer Clement, Edwidge Danticat, Cristina García, Stephanie Elizondo Griest, Andrea Thome, Helena Maria Viramontes

Aster(ix) print issues are usually published twice a year with additional content online. **Aster(ix)** is funded in part by the Dietrich School of Arts and Sciences and the Department of English at University of Pittsburgh.

Aster(ix) Journal

presents

10th Anniversary Issue
Part I: Poetry & Nonfiction

Edited by
Angie Cruz & Marta Lucía Vargas

April 2023

BLUE SKETCH PRESS | PITTSBURGH

ASTER(IX)—10th Anniversary Issue: Part I.

Individual acknowledgments available on pg. 200
Published via Blue Sketch Press, Pittsburgh.
www.bluesketchpress.com

10th Anniversary Issue: Part I
An Aster(ix) Anthology / Aster(ix) Journal
Edited by Angie Cruz—1st ed.

ISBN (print)   978-1-942547-20-4 (trade paperback)
                1-942547-20-6 (ISBN-10)

Cover art by Bogomil Mihaylov
Cover Design by Little Owl Creative

First Edition: June 2023

Printed in the United States of America
9 8 7 6 5 4 3 2 1

Contents

LETTER FROM
THE EDITOR

Angie Cruz & Marta Lucía Vargas

AKA an Aster(ix) 10th Year Anniversary Charla

Angie Cruz: Thank you for co-editing this issue with me. I can't believe we're celebrating the 10th year anniversary of Aster(ix) Journal. Remember that moment when we started the journal? We were on the phone: Nelly Rosario, Sheila Maldonado, Adriana Ramírez, Emily Raboteau, you and me. We were brainstorming the name for the journal and why we thought this project was important. The VIDA count had been released validating what we already knew, how women and BIPOC writers were underrepresented in mainstream literary spaces. That was the moment when we asked the question: why aren't we publishing what we love? And that night we named the journal. We were thinking about omissions and Adriana asked, "How about the word asterisk?" Then Sheila who was studying Mayan symbols suggested "ix" And I think it was you who offered the parenthesis.

Marta Lucía Vargas: I remember we were bringing in indigenous intelligence of what becomes language, and how language can be obliterated. How it can be massacred. And invented. So we were inventing. We were inventing our own language by creating this title that tried to capture everyone's essence. That was the beauty of it. A collaborative effort. It was a virtual platform to disseminate writing across the country, among us. The works that live in our printed issues and online are now scattered all over the world for love, for play, for art. We were creating a virtual republic for ourselves where we could gather and continue conversations. When I think of these ten years, I think, what does it mean to cumplir? It means to come through, to achieve. So this is 10 years of a project that has been realized. To cumplir is to be realized.

AC: Which is not that different from what we tried to do with WILL: Women in Literature & Letters back in 1997. We made a call for women of color writers to gather, read and write with us. We were thinking about the transformational possibility of literature. In the past ten years do you have some moments that you felt were particular to Aster(ix) where you understood the importance of the journal?

MLV: Big Question. I loved coming up with the title. It was like being in a birth. And then when our masthead of contributing editors and board members came together at Blue Mountain Center Retreat in 2016 to think and forward the agenda. That was a powerful experience for me. We discussed the online presence, the book presence, the actual objects that make up the journal and how we're trying to do different things. And people were coming up with different projects. A lot of things grew and were born there. That time was a great example of how we come together and we imagine ourselves into being. The essence of the work has always been what we love. And what we love could be content related. It could be context related. The root of it is how we allow our imaginations to run wild and free and turn them into something, take action.

AC: Which is really tied to the mission, right? I love how Aster(ix) has emerged into a laboratory, a space where we could play and experiment. It began with the naming of it, but also in the ways that we invite writers and artists to participate in play. The most exciting issues for me were the ones where we invited others to try something they wouldn't have otherwise unless we had made the invitation. I think of the Ferrante Project, where writers wrote anonymously. I think about the issue that you edited with Saretta Morgan and when we invited Jenlle Troxell to reimagine the modernist practice of the boudoir. Jenelle reminded us that we were part of a long tradition of literary magazines that were created by women with commitments to publish works on the margins. So Aster(ix) is part of a long literary tradition going back to the modernist era. with Jane Heap, and Margaret Anderson, where they rented out their apartment to fund The Little Review.

MLV: What happens when we feel safe and trusting in the unknown? Let us jump into the unknown and say what the fuck, let's just do it. Yeah, it doesn't matter whether it's in your apartment or at Blue Mountain, or by the edge of the water. It's this permission to be free. And recreate the center. We are the center, we are not the margin. Toni Morrison really described her life's work as recreating the center. It was a conscious decision to stand at the edge and make it the center.

AC: Yes, Morrison said, "I stood at the border. I stood at the edge and claimed it as central. I let the rest of the world move over to where I was." That quote embodies what we've been doing. Like the ways we continue to question language used in the realm of literary journals. Like what does it mean to "submit" work? Why do people have to submit? What is submission? Why not center an invitation to a conversation? Why are so many editors invested in claiming to discover someone? It's so colonialist! Why do we have to be the first to publish someone, why not reprint work? How can we bring new life to the work we love? We continue to have these conversations while editing together. Some of my favorite moments in our ten years have been when we edited together. When we were in cafes, reading poems closely and being in conversations about the line, line breaks, word choices. Not a lot of writers get that attentive editorial advice or guidance. But what's exciting for me is how we have become closer as a collective when we think through what we love and when we ask questions about the work.

MLV: The work is the play, play is the work. For my mother who was always moving, reading felt like being idle for her. If I'm reading, I'm available to move. I really didn't know this my entire life, my body knew it. So that's why I hid under the covers or in the library for hours. It was the protection of that action. When we grow up, we're among people who want to gather and do the things we used to do in the secret world. It's a secret society of work because no one is inviting us to do it anyway. But we have that urgency to do it and it's so powerful. It's overpowering. And we don't have a choice but to do it. And that's kind of cool.

AC: The truth is we're under no institutional obligation to meet deadlines for Aster(ix) and we often have to ask ourselves, why do we continue to do it. All of us have such demanding lives outside of Aster(ix) taking care of our children, elders, our writing, jobs to pay the rent, and yet when summoned we stay up at night pulling these issues together. So I ask you, what does it mean to continue to do this work? What compels you to continue to be part of this familia?

MLV: I remember being a naysayer of us back and saying, why are we doing this? Let's save some trees or some electricity. Do we have to do this? Should we just do our own work? And yes, yes, and yes. But it's powerful coming back together. The idea of coming together and nurturing each other to go wild. We are creating something that is necessary. It's not required by an institution, but it's required by our inner landscapes.

AC: I do think that even the diversity, aesthetics, walks of life, positionality,

of who has been influencing where the journal goes does create a vitality
to the work. Why do I continue doing the work? Every time I think about
quitting, I get an idea of another issue or project. So I guess I will continue
because I am still inspired by it. I'm also grateful that we have a vehicle to
put the ideas to work. For example, the "In Residence" column on our website
where we invited writers to respond to the lost painting, "Amaranta" by
Cecilia Vicuna. The writers we invited to participate were so thankful for the
prompt. For some it broke their writer's block or allowed them to flex a new
genre. So what excites me is to see what happens when we invite someone to
play and then see what they do.

MLV: This constant experimentation allows for a different kind of journal.
It's an amazing thing when we're working on an issue and people are
traveling, taking planes across the country and saying "what are we going
to make together here?" And sometimes, we don't know. And that's okay.
And that's acceptable. So, it's pretty radical, in the way that it's atypical in its
methodology and anti-capitalist. In terms of timeframe, deadlines. Even when
our fluidity may receive pushback.

AC: Historically, it has not always been easy to prioritize wellness over
deadlines and product. I believe that's what makes this largely volunteer run
effort sustainable– the ways that we offer flexibility to do the work without
pressure. Because if we would have put pressure on ourselves, I think a lot of
us would have quit. I see the journal as a conversation with you and everyone
on the board that is always emergent. The works are also in conversation with
each other. This is why I've always loved the ways Aster(ix) reprints old work,
because when you reprint something old and bring it with something new,
it becomes part of the new conversation and you can read it in a totally new
way.

*Marta Lucia Vargas and Angie Cruz met in 1996 in Taxco, Mexico
and soon after co-founded WILL Women and Literature & Letter,
with Adelina Anthony. WILL was a grassroots effort (1997-2001) with
a vision to gather women from all over the world who believed in the
transformative powers of reading and writing. Many of the writers who
participated in WILL are now contributors and a part of the Aster(ix)
masthead. In 2013, Adriana E. Ramírez co-founded Aster(ix) Journal
with Angie Cruz. with a commitment to pick up where WILL left off and
create a home for what we love, without explanation or apology.*

Originally published in our Fall 2016 issue, *What We Love*

Untitled & Ze

Amy Sara Carroll

S★★★★★★★★★★★★★★★★:
T★★★★★★★★★★★★★★★L
ARS IN A BOW
El Paso

ZE

All summer we set out to make an undocumentary. Rosa Alcalá taught me the word. I introduced myself to her because I love *Undocumentaries*. Our email messages were brief to one another. Mine were all fanfare, hers, gracious. Shyly in one of my messages I admitted that three years earlier Ricardo, Zé, and I had driven from Corpus Christi to San Diego. Stopping in El Paso, I'd wanted to invite her to have coffee with us. I'd wanted to call her out of the blue—something I never feel or do—without an introduction. Instead, because the night was dark and twinkling, I'd written a concave poem, "Stars in a bowl: El Paso." The next morning we walked into Ciudad Juárez. It was 2010. We went to a Sunday market that Ricardo had known as a child. Ricardo bought me a necklace of saints. I stumbled with Zé in the street. A nearby pedestrian helped me to my feet, blessed me, and told me to go home. That was six years ago when the Federal Police occupied the city, when the front page of its leading newspaper queried, "¿Qué quieren de nosotros?" This summer is haunted, but indifferent to rememory, as expanded cinema. I want to tell Rosa Alcalá that we filmed a "poet tree." Hanging from its branches were words like leaves. Fairy houses dotted its roots. Dulce and Zé built environments, dug holes and ditches, sculpted sundials so we'd always be able to tell time what we really think: it was the hour of my defeat but also hours of all things good and sweet, ungendered as our "No Movie" or Zé without his accent.

Amy Sara Carroll on "Untitled & Ze"

What do these pieces hold for you?

Untitled & Ze" project be/longing. The paired pieces are about building/sculpting environment-community; the crush of Rosa Alcalá's poetry ahead of Laura Harris's cultural theory ("undocument/aries"); my desire to find solace in the everyday, play, (my own) notched-entangled writing "ars in a bow."

Originally published in our Fall 2017 issue, *Dirty Laundry*

How To Search for Your Child

Norma Liliana Valdez

Colinas de Santa Fe, Veracruz, México

Drive a six-foot metal rod into the ground.
With each click-clack of the hammer,
dig the cross-shaped bar deeper into the soil.
Pull out the rod.
Bring it close to your nose.
Inhale. Wet earth or remains?
Exhume 253 bodies, none of them yours.
Yellow your skin.
Grow your hair waist-length.

Norma Liliana Valdez on "How to Search for Your Child"

Tell us about the history of this piece.

"How To Search For Your Child" is the convergence of a disappearance, two texts, and collective mobilization in the face of impunity called Colectivo Solecito.

A Disappearance.

In May of 2016, my tía Choncha's youngest brother, César González Lomelí, went missing in our family's hometown of San Gaspar de los Reyes, Jalisco. Though there were witnesses to the kidnapping, to date there has been no news of César's whereabouts or fate. For over a year after his disappearance, Choncha wouldn't eat much. How could she, not knowing if her brother had eaten? "Is he alive?" was an impossible question. The lack of nourishment led to a temporary yellowed pigmentation of the skin. She'd also promised God not to cut her hair until he was returned.

The Texts.

In 2016, JD Pluecker translated Sara Uribe's *Antígona González*, a complex, hybrid narrative of a woman looking for her brother's body. I read the book in one sitting. Then read it again. One body became hundreds, then thousands. Each body, César's. Each body, someone's beloved. On May 10th, 2017, *The New York Times* published an article describing the methods used by Colectivo Solecito, a group of women (mostly mothers) in search of their disappeared.

Colectivo Solecito.

The first three lines of the poem, "Drive a six-foot metal rod into ground / With each click-clack of hammer / dig the cross-shaped bar deeper into soil" describe the photo under the NYT headline. In it, Martha González Menéndez and Rosario Sáyago Montoya, members of Colectivo Solecito, search for the remains of their beloveds in a mass grave in Colinas de Santa Fe, Veracruz. A second photo shows Martha inhaling the scent of the rod. Colectivo Solecito searches and finds when governmental bodies refuse to do so.

Poetry

Originally published in our Spring 2016 issue, *Atravesando*

Calling Collect from Prison/Father-Daughter Intermediary

Amy Elizabeth Bishop

:::: Tell her
  Tuesdays are good days —I know
 making time is hard. Make sure she is reading
  —make sure she stays
in school; tell her
    keep your nails ragged as an architect's
   first skyline to serrate
  bodies that want
to claim you, as if claiming is all
   they know how to do.
Teach her to throw a punch:
  remember to leave
 your thumb exposed—she'll learn
   after the first time she breaks
      a knuckle.
       :::: Tell her:
how we buried baby teeth/first
 haircut/christening clothes in a prayer

chest. How precious   how adored   how
many hours on our knees—
          Tell her   —send
a school picture to show
—to fall asleep with—
          smile like waking   to birthday/Christmas mornings.
Tell her I would turn
      this world color-blind
          for her :::: don't tell her how much I miss
      her/don't tell I called/don't tell

Originally published in our Winter 2019-2020 issue, *The Poetry Issue*

Sequence from Botanic América

Christina Olivares

sparrows void sneaker hollows
thrown over a telephone line
with nests. at dusk

> we are little, crowded
> in a backseat, dirt-funky and
> playing the quiet

game. we break when we spy
mcdonald's, glow singing us singing
back as a lady in front wavers high

> high high: it's always apocalypsing.
> apocalypse: riddled earth body tilts
> as it sprouts us, in this
> home-land a homeland to us
> our america, an

unpracticed parent
unparalleled lover

(later: her body as mine,
shock of a love: discovering there was this growing thing in us both)

    like: the burning of a body when it is touched
    like: the burning of a home when it is touched

        exhibit a: the land which can be done upon and to
            exhibit b: a series of encounters with desire
                exhibit c: language

    tell me how many words
    do you come from?
a love song to a place
    a place that is queer
a love song to a place of queerness

        a love song to queers

            a love song to queers I love

I speak in unfamiliar languages
none mine
        ausente como

are we imaginable?

        what   do

                        our

                   these

                           children imagine?

The summer I dreamt a pony at the door
and I woke up

                    my small awed hands poking

in the dusk light squared

                    above and so eagerly

wishing for the being I dreamed.

                    I check, breathless,

                    all ripe want. For me. Also for us.

No pony:

        what's a pony to a girlchild in the projects?
        a regurgitated dream?
        a fever dream of your best girl self?
        beautiful, hot, to the touch,
        unoriginal?   can you
        be good enough for one
        to appear for you– first you, then
        the dream of the queer animal you are
        afraid to be, such good,
        good girls both?

I say to Bronx burned —

        what I am sure of is
        we ate its earth as children: a transfer of desiring.
        silky-threaded little bodies plus
        burned land's milky sustaining
        coding and becoming in us
        a redressed burning– a desire in it as us
        to be ever more and more embodied,
        redolent.   a burned earth resituated
        and made new again in our
        little new bodies, a

queer love song:

different america built itself inside of us, a botanical
no america, inverse that survived,   made new

america   home land.
If a child   consumes dirt, what new does the child become?
Children   of the americas eat earth because they are hungry:
farce of scarcity.   Different kinds of hunger. Our knowledges
are also loosely archived,   tightly archived, hidden away,
oh america   a fever
dream edging delight   an archive of grief thickly
                                    renders us
                       we remember ourselves
vaguely,
    as if we and not this are/is the dream of   america.

Originally published in our Spring 2014 issue,
Ra(i)ces: Black Feminist Encounters

What the Ground Remembers

Courtney Desiree Morris

1.

The dead speak to me. Cluster around my bed and crowd my sleep, filling my dreams with memories that are not mine. These ancestors insist that there must be a vessel, a witness. Before I am born they run their fingers like chalk over my forehead, brush them over my palms, my tongue. There will be a witness.

This daughter will remember.

2.

República Dominicana
Boca de Nigua
1796.

The sugar mill is burning. The overseers lie motionless on the ground, desecrated, their lifeless bodies soaked with the scarlet stain of their own blood. In life, they were cruel, pushing the enslaved workers in the mill to exhaustion. The fires and filthy fumes of the sugar mill never ceased. The consumption of European markets required that the labor never end. Working constantly from dusk until dawn, the enslaved Africans who powered the *ingenio* at Boca de Nigua, laid the foundations for the wealth of the Spanish Empire and the birth of the modern global capitalist order.

The hazards of the job were many: Workers lost limbs harvesting cane, grinding cane, boiling cane. They grunted alongside oxen pulling the cane press, the stench of sweating bodies and burnt cane filling the sugar mill. Like farm animals, their lives were miserable and short, lasting an average of only seven years upon arrival to the New World. Children did not live here, could not survive the violence of the cane fields. Stolen from their homes and thrust into a brutal labor system these Yoruba, these Congo, these Asante, these Coromantee, these Fulani, these Akan, became the faceless mass of black laborers whose bodies fertilized the soil that produced the first truly global industry.

The violence of Boca de Nigua is legendary. Overseers routinely brutalize the workers, using tactics of physical and psychological torture – sexual terror and murder – to discipline a resentful and recalcitrant labor force. At Boca de Nigua sexual violence is a routinized way of life. It is pervasive, ravaging everyone in its path. The Spanish overseers use their cocks like weapons, sodomizing male and female enslaved alike. Rape is a common act, a tactic designed to break the worker into total submission.

Runaways are tortured and branded. Rebels are executed and dismembered, their torn limbs hung throughout the colony to serve as warning to others who might be similarly inspired to resist. The brutality, however, does little to subordinate the enslaved Africans brought to the *ingenio*. Rather they stoke their resentments in private amongst each other, away from the ever-watchful eyes of their enslavers and the observant ears of potential traitors within their ranks. They organize themselves slowly, gaining the trust of their companions, recruiting new members to the project. Memory fuels survival, stokes rebellion. These children of the sun toil endlessly under its gaze and the scrutiny of stone-hearted men and they wait.

The tiny island of Hispaniola belongs to the ancestors. The soil holds their blood, their bodies, their memory. When history refuses to account for them, the ground remembers.

Inspired by the rumors of rebellion wafting into the country from the western half of the island, the enslaved workers of Boca de Nigua unleash a wave of retribution on the Spanish colonial government. When the smoke clears, the rebels form their own collective government and, foreshadowing the birth of the world's first Black republic next door, declare themselves sovereign and free of any colonial power.

Their freedom is short lived. The seven leaders of the collective government, including a woman named Ana María, are taken to the capital where they are tortured and then quartered. Their severed heads are hung at the gates of the colonial city for 10 days. The Spanish are particularly fond of dismemberment as a punishment because they believe that this ensures that the souls of these African rebels will not rest.

I think, perhaps they have miscalculated.

Indeed, our souls cannot rest. There is far too much work still to be done.

3.

Belle Glade, Florida.
February 2013

Sugar is on my mind a lot these days.

State Road 80 from West Palm Beach to Belle Glade knifes through the uniform terrain of southeast Florida. Belle Glade sits in the heart of the muck, the swath of fertile, pitch-black, mineral-rich soil that sustains the sea of sugarcane surrounding the towns on the edges of Lake Okeechobee. Sugar cane grows in either side of this local highway, swaying languidly in the warm, humid breeze. The sugar cane are hypnotic, they hold the gaze with their repetitious movement, seeming to wave in greeting. The eye likes clean lines and repetition. I try to remember to keep my eyes on the road and away from the cane. My father has warned me to be careful of this road; the canals that run alongside it hold the bodies of too many people lulled to distraction by the monotony of the landscape. I keep both eyes open as I drive west, occasionally diverting my attention from the road to follow the dense pewter wall of smoke circling into the sky as the cane fields burn. The fields are always on fire, the harvest never ends.

South Florida is cane country. The first governor of Spanish Florida, Pedro Menéndez de Avilés, tried unsuccessfully to grow imported sugarcane there and there is evidence to suggest that native peoples in the region may have engaged in small-scale sugarcane cultivation. By the 1560s, sugar had already become a global commodity, a luxury that only the very rich could afford – access to sugar functioned as a sign of wealth. They say that Queen Elizabeth loved sugar so much that she ate it until her teeth were blackened, rotting stumps. Even then this sweet, granular concoction had the power to drive people out of their heads. The emergence of the *ingenio*, or the sugar mill, as the first model of pre-industrial mass production meant, however, that soon sugar would become a luxury that the entire world could afford.

Despite repeated failures in the Everglades, white settlers kept coming, bringing their dreams of fortune, power, and access to cheap, abundant land with them. By the late 19th century, South Florida was still a wilderness of marshy, swampland. The Seminole call the Glades *pahay-okee*, or "grassy water," for the sea of endless sharp, double-edged sawgrass that grew wild in the shallow bed of water spreading southward from Lake Okeechobee down to the tip of the peninsula. When the Seminoles refused to leave these lands after the purchase of the Florida territory from Spain in 1819, President Andrew Jackson plunged the region into a series of "Seminole Wars" that lasted well into the 1830s. Even when their leader, the famed guerrilla leader, Osceola was captured and executed during the Second Seminole War, the Seminoles resisted, retreating deeper into the labyrinthine waterways and the darkness of the Everglades, emerging periodically to attack forts, loot food supplies from soldiers and civilians, and slaughter anyone unfortunate or foolish enough to be caught in their path. But the Seminoles were subjugated, among the first casualties of Manifest Destiny. This campaign of ethnic cleansing, displacement, and conquest was considered a success — despite the presence of living Seminole peoples today. Yet Seminole peoples exist in public memory only as a colorful tribe of people, whose likenesses have been reduced to football mascots, the names of their leaders affixed to abject public structures like housing projects, prisons, and dying towns whose futures hold no promise.

It is estimated that approximately 1500 soldiers died in the Second Seminole War that drove out most of the Seminoles; *there is no record of Seminole deaths.*

The conquest of South Florida made sugar possible. By the early 1920s, whites began to settle in significant numbers in the region. Their settlement accompanied the effort to subdue the very landscape of the region, and the federal government funded projects to drain the Everglades. The drainage exposed hundreds of thousands of acres of silty, black muck, whose agricultural capacities became the stuff of legend. The land, however, was not always obedient. The drainage dried out the exposed topsoil, turning it into dust that imprinted itself on everything and everyone. Everglades residents soon learned that the land would ignite like a matchstick at the slightest provocation leading to subterranean fires that burned for months on end. The ground became an animal: a living thing seething with rage.

Right around the time that the U.S. Sugar Corporation was formed — creating what would become the largest domestic sugar operation in the country, with 100,000 acres devoted to cane cultivation and 6,000 employees to process it all — Janie and Tea Cake, the lead characters in Zora Neale Hurston's 1937 novel, *Their Eyes Were Watching God,* were also making their way to the muck in search of good work and good times. I was in high school the first time I read *Their Eyes Were Watching God* and was shocked when I realized that someone had written a novel about a place that I knew. Driving across the muck, Janie's first impression of the Everglades returns to me:

...Everything in the Everglades was big and new. Big Lake Okeechobee, big beans, big cane, big weeds, big everything. Weeds that did well to grow waist high up the state were eight and often ten feet tall down there. Ground so rich that everything went wild. Volunteer cane just taking the place. Dirt roads so rich and black that half a mile of it would have fertilized a Kansas wheat field. Wild cane on either side of the road hiding the rest of the world. People wild too. [1]

Poor white trash, Negroes, and Caribbean labor migrants poured into the labor camps of the Everglades, transforming it from a vast swamp into a farming paradise where the soil gave away its sweetness like the loose women who roamed the streets of Colored Town in Belle Glade. The workers braved the sawgrass whose serrated blades sliced their flesh open like raw meat, they endured the muck that worked its way into their clothing and irritated their skin. They drank, they gambled, they partied, they screwed around, had families, went to church, and sometimes someone died in a juke joint brawl. But mostly they worked from can't see to can't see, waiting for their weekly pay so that they could live like kings again if only for a night. Sugar was big business and the growers raked in such immense profits, banks established a rotating check cashing system so that there would not be a run on the banks on payday. Black labor, bodies and sweat carried out the reclamation of the Everglades and laid the foundations for the rise of Big Sugar in the 1960s.

When a category 5 hurricane slammed into Lake Okeechobee on September 14, 1928, claiming more than 2,500 lives in an hour, it destroyed this unequal paradise. Lake levels had been rising steadily all summer with the record-breaking rates of rainfall. The hurricane devastated Puerto Rico, Guadeloupe and the Leeward Islands before winding its way northwest to Florida. Jim Crow reigned in the Glades, shaping the racial geography of the region through residential segregation and racially dividing public space. While wealthier white families lived within the towns of Clewiston, Belle Glade, South Bay, and Pahokee, black migrant laborers and their families were compelled to live on the low-lying, flood prone shores of Lake Okeechobee. When the hurricane came, they had nowhere to run and many waited in their homes, their eyes watching God, praying for a deliverance that did not come. The storm made no distinction among its targets but in death, as in life, black and white must never meet. In Belle Glade, Black bodies were thrown into a mass grave just outside the city and burned; caskets were scarce and reserved for white victims.

When my grandfather, Rennick Carlton Morris, Sr., came to the United States in the 1950s as a cane cutter, the getting on the muck was still good. After the storm of 1928, sugar emerged as the region's most important cash crop. Sugar was resilient, could withstand days of underwater submersion, and thrived in the fecund black soil. The problem lay with harvesting. Until mechanization, sugar cane required intense manual labor and increasingly Florida growers relied on unorganized, imported labor to get the job done. The poor white folks and Negro migrant workers who had flooded the Glades each season in search of work began to make demands on their employers. The Jamaican Guest Worker program was the state's response to poor people trying to leverage their labor power against capital. In the years following World War II, thousands of workers from Jamaica, St. Kitts, Barbados, and the Bahamas migrated on seasonal contracts to cut cane on the muck. My grandfather was among these workers.

He came as a young man with a new family to provide for. His skills as a mechanic – which he'd picked up after lying about his age to enlist in the British Royal Air Force – enabled him to quickly move up the ranks from cane cutter to supervisor. Cane cutting was dirty, miserable, dangerous work. Many a cane cutter had lost an ear, a finger, or a limb to the fields as they swung their machetes in a firm, swift arc towards the body in order to leave a clean cut at the cane stalk's base. Sometimes, delirious with thirst and fatigue, a cutter would swing his machete too hard and the blade would hit the cane stalk and bounce back in its owner's direction. Missing limbs and lacerations on the head, upper body, and torso bore testimony to the violence of the work. To quench their thirst they would slice the cane on top, which held the freshest juice, and suck on the sweet fiber. Eating the sweet pieces on the bottom would only leave a man thirsty and desperate. They could not afford to rest. Stragglers and those who failed to meet quota could be sent home for the day, or, worse, sent back to Jamaica, empty-handed.

After paying for food, which came directly out of their paychecks, the men scraped their meager savings together to send back to waiting families in the Caribbean. Those dollars sent children to school to become doctors, lawyers, teachers, ministers, nurses. Workers built up and expanded their homes one room at a time, season by season. In 1972, after years of slowly immigrating his family one child, niece, and cousin at a time, he brought all of his children to the United States, with papers, to a tiny home in the tiny town of South Bay. His sugar dream had paid off.

My family, like so many immigrant families from the Caribbean, left their home countries to build new homes here. Heading west into the small city of Belle Glade, visitors are greeted by a Disneyesque welcome sign: *Belle Glade: Her soil is her fortune*. That may have been true at one time and maybe it still is for the handful of wealthy families that own the cane fields surrounding the town. For everyone else, Belle Glade is now a town in decline. When Big Sugar mechanized in the early 1990s, thousands of Jamaican, Haitian, Mexican, and African-American workers were left without work or the promise of future employment. Instead of jobs, they got crack cocaine, two new prisons, and catastrophic rates of HIV/AIDS infection that transformed Belle

Glade overnight into the "AIDS capital of the United States."

My Pop died in 1988 right around the same time that the sugar dream died on the muck. People from all over the Glades came to pay their respects at his funeral at the Church of God of South Bay. The swollen crowd tumbled outside of the tiny church filling the parking lot and spilling over into the street. He had become something of a statesman in South Bay, a community elder who helped everyone who came across his path. He was a hard, authoritative man, with enormous hands and seemingly endless strength. But in the end, even he proved finite. The consensus was clear: Mr. Morris was a good man who had worked himself to death to give his family a better life.

Pop is buried, along with my grandmother and Uncle Oral, in Foreverglades Mausoleum Gardens at the intersection of Ice Plant Road and W. Sugar House Road. They rest under the watchful gaze of what my people call Big Sugar: the Sugar Cane Growers Co-op. The graveyard is surrounded by wild sugar cane that towers precariously around its carefully manicured boundaries. If the cane were allowed to run freely it would overtake the small graveyard in a matter of mere months. From my grandparents' gravesite I watch the smoke from Big Sugar spiral towards the heavens. Sugar has always run our lives. Sugar brought us to the Everglades, made our lives possible here, and then eventually made it impossible to stay here. It moves us still, taking us under duress to sites not of our own choosing or our making.

The sugar house and its dirty fumes shrink in my rearview mirror as I leave the cemetery heading east back to West Palm Beach. Gregory Isaac's satin tenor fills the tiny car and we sing together, "I was given as a sacrifice/to build a black man's hell/and a white man's paradise/but now that I know/It's time, I've got to go Lord/the proceedings seem so painful/and so slow, slow, slow…" I drive and I don't look back. I keep both my eyes on the road.

4.

República Dominicana
Boca de Nigua
March 2013

It is silent in Boca de Nigua. A lonely cow grazes aimlessly in the field, observing our movements through the ruins with mild interest. The mill is a hollowed shell of itself. Graffiti litters the walls. Local residents use the area to hang out, drink, and meet for romantic trysts. There is no marker to remind us that we are on sacred ground; that no matter who we are or where we come from, we all share ancestral ties to this remote corner of the Dominican Republic. Eight out of ten Africans trafficked through the Américas entered here, labored here, died here. People who wore my face were here. Memory lives here.

Our tour guide is a round, exuberant Mestiza anthropologist. A feminist, a mystic, a scholar, she outlines – in all of its ugly brutality- the colonial world of Boca de Nigua. I am listening to her, but my mind is somewhere else. The breeze settles cold and uneasy on my exposed arms. The air tastes metallic in my mouth. I am looking for, seeing myself in this place, my people in this place. The sorrow burrows into my womb and curls in on itself. Fear forms a small knot in my belly and I do not need the tour guide to tell me what my body already knows, what the ground remembers. The knowledge is saturating my senses, the ancestors whispering insistently into my ears, their breath running down my spine and gently lifting the hair on the back of my neck.

They want me to know they are here.

Our guide tells us that despite the unspeakable number of Africans who died in this place no bodies have ever been recovered. Some Africans, desperate and knowing they would never again see their homes in their lifetime, take matters and mortality into their own hands. They choose to crucify the flesh and fly home to Guinea. Spaniards dismissed the suicides as the logical behavior of deranged, primitive peoples; they are more impressed by these Africans' indomitable will to live. But they still die. Causes of death: rebellion, illness, exhaustion, torture, grief.

Despite all of their searching, archaeologists are unable to locate their bodies. They know when they stumble across Spaniards because their bodies bear the signs of Christianity: rosaries, appropriate clothing, and small bibles. Scholars speculate that perhaps Africans were buried alongside whites — that is, if they were baptized. Others think perhaps Spanish slaveholders tossed their bodies into the angry sea. But there is no proof of this. I ponder this, smell the salty air, and remember all of the Africans lying on the bottom of the Atlantic Ocean, resting in Olokun's arms.

Or maybe they simply flew away.

My father tells me a story of a recurring dream he has had since he was a little boy. At night, he spreads his arms and takes flight, soaring into the heavens, taking in the tiny green island below him. He flies over mountains and bush, dunes and forests, twirling through the trees, the spicy scent of sage and fevergrass filling his lungs. When he wakes up, he is exhausted and his arms hurt. His face is filled with wonder as he tells me this story.

They say we eat too much salt and that is why these new world Africans cannot fly. I imagine the sugar weighs us down, too.

5.

1998: Dominican archaeologists find the remains of an enslaved African beneath a cathedral in colonial Santo Domingo. They know he was enslaved because he is buried with manacles on his wrists, the better to serve his masters in the after life, I suppose. When the Archbishop of Santo Domingo learns of this find, he orders that the site be covered over with cement and the archaeologist who discovered it is promptly fired.

2006: A Mexican construction crew in Campeche unearths the remains of some 180 people in a churchyard cemetery. Four of these are later confirmed to be of West African origin. This is determined by the chemical composition and sharpened points of their teeth. Located on the edge of the Gulf of Mexico, Campeche was one of colonial Mexico's richest port cities. One of the earliest slave ports, the traffic in Africans at Campeche swelled as the sugar industry grew throughout Latin America. Archaeologists surveying the site say it will provide us with a more thorough understanding of the diminished physical health of enslaved Africans in the Americas. I am surprised that they seem to need this additional proof.

6.

I wander the grounds of Boca de Nigua, feeling for all my life like a ghost. Touching the walls, the ground, staring into the empty blue sky. The earth smells of manure, damp and heavy. I inhale it deeply, let it ease into my lungs.

After our guide completes her tour, our group fans out across the grounds, sorting out our feelings, trying to make sense of the magnetic pull that has brought each of us here. I touch the base of the crushing mill, see Africans grinding the cane alongside oxen, coated with sweat from the heat of the furnace. I walk the grounds as a free woman and remember the ancestors who took their lives and bodies somewhere else to escape the misery of slavery.

The land is rapidly reclaiming one building. Sleeping quarters? Wood planks jut out from the walls like the fronds of a woven basket. I tiptoe around the building, inexplicably afraid to enter, but I do. On my way out, I reach down and pocket a shard of broken red brick. In Jamaica, they say you should never take anything from a graveyard, because the spirit of the deceased will follow you home.

I take the brick.

7.

In the quiet of my home, I light sage, pour water, set white flowers on clean white cloth. I invite the ancestors to speak to me. I wait and I listen.

Endnotes:
[1] Zora Neale Hurston. 1990 [1937]. *Their Eyes Were Watching God.* New York: Harper and Row Publishers. 123.

Originally published in our Fall 2022 issue, *Mothers Unearthed*

Seasonal Affective Disorder

Marie Myung-Ok Lee

There's a certain smell I associate with fall, a crispness that carries melancholy. These fleeting whiffs emerge in the heat of August in flashes, like heat lightning, so quick you can't tell if it was an olfactory mirage. Subnotes of grasses drying and going to seed. Of trees informed by the length of days, sending out the invisible signal to their leaves to withdraw the chlorophyll that will leave only color behind. In New York City, there's the subtle ganky tang of gingko nuts crushed underfoot. But the smell recalls the same memory: I am in sixth grade, getting my new school supplies ready, covering my books with brown bags from Red Owl.

My son was born in the winter of the new millennium, when a faction of people thought the changeover to "00" would cause planes to fall out of the sky, for clocks to stop. The clocks didn't stop, but the climate change—the threat of which fossil fuel harvesting corporations have known about since as early as 50 years ago and have done nothing but hide that information in order to pursue profits—accelerated. That bill is starting to come due. Everyone was on Twitter yesterday watching footage of a seaside house being washed away by a risen ocean. The news was careful to state not once but twice that the house was unoccupied. I.e., nothing to see here, no one was hurt. Again glossing over the fact a lot of us, the younger people disproportionately, are going to be hurt. Escaping climate change is not as easy as making sure you are not home when the sea comes for your house.

For my son, the fall doesn't have a consistent smell. Some days we have leaves falling and budding at the same time, confused crocuses poking up out of the humus.

* * *

Fall is considered to be the Korean nation's favorite season. This mad love for the season that twins beauty and death appeared back when I first ventured into learning my mother tongue via night classes at NYU. Our Korean 101 textbook read: "Of all the seasons, Koreans think fall is the most beautiful."

One hears this sentiment all the time in Korea. It was new to me to think of a country, a people, having a favorite season— melancholy as part of its beauty. In the west, we seek the positive emotion, we do all we can to avoid the negative, which is probably why it's easy to receive and absorb the comforting lies of climate change denial.

I was born in Hibbing, Minnesota, a town of around 16,000. Resource extraction is its primary industry. The town had already, however, depleted most of the iron mines while I was still a child. I would hear all the old miners complaining about China undercutting the market, while our in-class filmstrips showed that no, all the ore geologists thought was unlimited, had already been dynamited out of the ground. We were told of a time that scientists felt the huge, vast ocean could swallow up all the excess carbon we produced starting from the industrial revolution. But in this, too, humans are too good at exceeding expectations for environmental destruction.

* * *

Winter of course was the primary season for people in Hibbing. Bob Dylan, who also grew up in my town, marveled in his memoir at the length and breadth of the unrelenting cold, the unending blanket of white—to the point one would start to hallucinate. The smell of burning wood evokes atavistic relaxation at the thought of a warm orange light; other human bodies gathering, hands unfurling toward the warmth.

But I remember more a crystalline freshness, almost an absence of scent, but not quite. My spouse is always impressed when I open our NYC apartment's window and declare it will snow. It always does. I can smell the flurries in the air before the flakes fall. It's a certain humidity— subtler—that I can catch when it's about to fall from battleship-gray clouds.

As with climate change, with such an unrelenting season, the western approach was to ignore or obfuscate. The "cool" thing to do was to blast the heat in your car and wear shorts all winter long. I remember in elementary school my mother making me wear clunky snow boots and being ridiculed by the other children. I took ice skating lessons, where we were made to wear short little dresses, flesh colored tights. A sweater, or even mittens, would have been laughed at. I used to hate skating practice. I'm not sure why my mother was so insistent on me and my sister taking lessons. We even had to take them in the summer, where the indoor rink would be just as miserably cold.

* * *

In the West we tend to mark the change of the seasons by somewhat egotistical measurements. There's a feeling of indignance in the Winter Solstice, when the sun is the furthest away from us and that day is the shortest, compared to the summer when it's the closest.

In Korea, there are beautiful poetic signposts. Dae borum is the first Full Moon after The New Year. There is another notation for "Enter spring." Even Buddha's birthday, Seokga tansinil, occurs on day 8 of month 4 on the lunar calendar, which means April or May. Every full moon is the 15th of the lunar month; I was charmed while watching the popular translated K Drama, *Hospital Playlist*, when one of the characters, Songhwa, looks up and sees the full moon and says, "I didn't know it was the 15th!" in the same way we'd say, "I can't believe it's June already!" The seemingly less stable lunar calendar is logical and primary in Korea.

When I was living in Korea for a Fulbright and working at an unwed mothers' home, I participated in a kimjang, a late-autumn ritual of mass outdoor production of kimchi for winter. With an almost shamanistic determination that the weather was about to turn cold, intersecting with estimations of the cheapest price for Asian cabbage, one day or two or three are spent in different outdoor spaces. It's not all done on a specific day but is more like the intermittent synchrony of fireflies. You'll just know when it's time.

In Seoul or the countryside you'll see men hauling mountains of cabbage brought in by farmers' truckload, the women laughing and gossiping while carefully cleaning the cabbages and soaking them in brine, preparing the fillings over the hours it takes for the cabbage leaves to properly soften. There are special tubs the size of children's wading pools to clean the cabbage. In the Seoul alley where I lived, the aunties used clean trash cans.

The job I was given for the kimjang was to peel the ginger, probably because little could go wrong with that. Still, an impatient auntie was aghast at how my whittling technique was wasting so much flesh. She grabbed my paring knife and showed me how to hold it perpendicular in order to scrape off the barest micro-layer of ginger-skin, to dig out between the appendage-like knobs as meticulously as one might wash between a baby's fingers.

In America, access to ingredients has changed so much by modern technologies—we can get watermelon year round. In Korea, daily food life, such as the preparation of kimchi, has not changed all that much since the Joseon Dynasty. The only sign of modernization in this timeless ritual was the use of a hose to wash away the effluvia of red pepper, shrimp paste, garlic skins into the gutter. At the end, each of us were gifted plastic bags full of kimchi, the housewives transferred them to a traditional nut-brown clay onggi on their tiny city balconies to ferment.

Richer people have separate kimchi refrigerators that, like a wine cooler, keep it at a correct temperature: cold, but not freezing, not unlike the genius tradition of burying the onggi in the earth, which would also keep it at the right temperature, no matter the ambient temperature. The fermentation process preserves the vitamin C in the cabbage in storage, to nourish its eaters through a Korean winter, powered by winds from Siberia, just as long and as cold as anything in Hibbing.

My kimchi is salad-fresh but also funky with heaping scoops of salted shrimp, a bright red from the hot pepper. As my plastic bags ferment in my tiny office-tel one-room, it mellows into the kimchi I know. I eat heaps of it with rice, make a tofu stew when the weather turns cold. It's so good that it doesn't even last me to the sour phase when it's delightful for fried rice.

I praise the ingenuity of my ancestors, resetting my cultural frame, remembering how my father restrained himself from eating kimchi when he was working (which, as the lone anesthesiologist in an isolated town, was often). Most people in our small town did not know what tofu was, much less kimchi, but the few who knew of it did not make favorable faces. My mother wouldn't let us kids eat it, as she was worried about the smell and being bullied. The only other time I came across a reference to kimchi was when our babysitter was watching MASH, and the GIs saw some Koreans burying what is mistaken to be bombs ground, only for it to turn out to be even more dangerous in the western conception: smelly, funky kimchi.

* * *

The first signs of spring loosen the snow, the way the shortening days of fall loosen the leaves on the trees. We kids were delighted when spring really got going, the snowmelt would form miniature rivers and the smallest children tried to fish in these streams. We would build dams, sail paper boats, running along with them downhill. The other side was undeveloped "dumps" where wild prairie grass had somehow managed to grow, even though our hill was constructed from old iron mine tailings. Overturn a rock and you'd see not soil, but orange-red ore. Walking there would turn the soles of your sneakers a bright red. In the dumps, snowmelt pooled and formed temporary lakes.

I remember the delight when the first pussywillows appeared at the "lakes" fringed by cattails, those velvet hotdogs on sticks swaying in the wind. How, as the days lengthened, the soft fur of the pussywillows would give way to green knobs that would unfurl into leaves, the lakes grew smaller, the cattails would swell, like grandma's antique sofa busting out foam at the seams. The smell of late spring, the heaviness of pollen, the hints of a hot summer, would smell of sex and reproduction setting off a happy restlessness that was almost unbearable.

* * *

With the warming earth, I wonder how kimjang will be affected, the erratic highs and lows, instead of the gradual, predictable march to winter. Will that affect the growth of cabbage? Will the warming earth render this backup method of storage obsolete? Unlike Americans, who laugh away weather extremes by frying eggs on car hoods and tweeting about it, Koreans note the unmistakable patterns, the climb of the yearly records. On the Korean news I see anxious headlines, "Weather forecaster warns of disappearing spring and fall," i.e., the weather is very cold and very hot and nothing, really, in between. The emotion of these headlines, unlike anything I ever see in the US, also grips me with dread and grief for what is already irrevocably broken, and what is to come.

In the US, we don't seem to react to the consequences of our own human assault on the natural world. In the Pacific northwest, mussels boil alive in their own shells. In our Minnesota neighbor, Canada, 500 people died in a heat wave this past June. The first climate change illness lawsuit was filed by a woman whose health—asthma and other ailments—have been caused by this new, wrong climate. In Minneapolis, where my mother lives, the streets have often buckled with heat in the summer— but also, now, in the winter, with cold.

I think about my son, who has autism and intellectual disability. If you ask him, "today is Monday, what is tomorrow?" he'll pick one from the slot machine in his head. This, I get. The seven day week is a product of industrialization, the work week. I am realizing that the wonderful thing about Korea's reliance on natural cycles, like the doctors in my K drama, means that even the most western-seeming people still keep track of the Lunar calendar, which forces you to look up into the sky. There are also no "leftover" days, like Leap Year, which need to be jimmied back in. Days progress, each erasing the last, with no remainders—going forward yet also circling back with the seasons.

When I ask my son, born into the new century, what season it is, he guesses. I try to give him mnemonics: Fall is when the leaves *fall*. Yet, it's almost eighty degrees out, I am sweating in my office, and people outside walk by in sandals and shorts, a few in season-appropriate down jackets, but slung over their arms or unzipped. The leaves similarly seem to be hedging. Many decide not to leave the tree, until, instead of coloring, they just fall off green, in slightly rotten wads. What I thought was a massive color change on the mountains when I was in Aspen in September was actually a climate-change related fungal disease in pine trees that was turning the needles golden. The aspens were still green.

I think of the three years when my best friend was dying of cancer, how flying into Asheville was often stymied by various odd and extreme weather systems, how many texts I sent to her of weather delayed flight—how one day in late spring as I taught my class before heading to the airport, the clear afternoon suddenly darkened, the window we had wide open to the spring breezes suddenly filled with swirling drifts of snow, the students staring at my wheelie bag as if themselves wondering if I was going to make it, where I was going, as the wind screamed and the students struggled to shut the window.

When I went to Asheville for a last time for her memorial service, the road to the venue was dangerously, newly flooded, and I almost didn't make it.

* * *

I suspect my son's disinterest in the seasons is part of his intellectual disability. But also, like any neurotypical people his age and below, it is possible he doesn't have a concept of seasons.

A few years ago at my high school reunion, I wanted to talk about climate change with my classmates. Growing up, Hibbing often made the national news in winter with jolly weatherman Willard Scott oohing about the negative temperatures in "America's icebox." Now, Hibbing has once again gained fame as the epicenter of climate change, an avatar of a phenomenon the National Climate Assessment labels a "polar switch": colder areas warming even more quickly than warmer ones; our town experiences the largest temperature difference in warming temperatures over its 1906-1960 average.[1]

But classmates tell me to shut up, hurry and get drunk.

Now the seasons don't smell like seasons. When I take pandemic walks with my son to the Harlem piers, the tang of gingko is just as often the tang of an ominous rot odor emanating from the sewer grates, even in the middle of "winter" (the quotes marking that it's often 60-70 degrees). From time to time, it smells like monsoon season in Korea— but that also is not a smell of seasons, because Korea has monsoons, and New York City does not (or should not). But now we have climate change rains that seem like someone is pouring water straight from the sky from a huge bucket.

In fall, the leaves are never as crisp.

I want to make my son apple cider doughnuts but it's hard to get in the mood when I'm sweating.

My son often says, "It is Mommy's job to keep me safe."

I am deeply moved by this trust, I take it as an "I love you." He is dependent on me to protect him, and nothing makes me feel more helpless and sad than thinking of leaving him some day to this boiled-mussel hellscape. It's because of him that I won't stop talking about, reminding people what we've lost—with more to continue to lose.

As mothers we bring life into this world, but the even bigger question remains: what kind of life—and death—will we be consigning our children to, if we don't take action? If we don't try to reverse the very course we have set ourselves upon?

-

Endnotes:

[1] Rising Temperatures (2014, May 7). *The New York Times.* https://www.nytimes.com/interactive/2014/05/06/us/Rising-Temperatures.html

Marie Myung-Ok Lee on "Seasonal Affective Disorder"

Rereading this piece, what does it bring to mind for you?

The New York Times recently ran an abhorrently promotional feature on Elizabeth Koch, who until that piece was known mostly for being the financial source for the literary journal Catapult. Few in the literary world noted she was of "that" Koch family, her father being one of the most powerful climate change enablers/profiteers of this century. (One reason for this obscurity was that during her MFA, Koch lied, saying she wasn't from "that" family).

I admired the work in Catapult and occasionally considered submitting there, but always held back for some reason. When asked by Emily Raboteau, a writer and activist I admire, to contribute a piece that combined mothering and climate change to Asteri(x), I jumped at the chance all the more because those two issues—essential as they are to human life--tend not to be considered "literary" by journals.

I had long wanted to write a piece combining disparate, desperate thoughts I had about changing world, how it would affect my son, who is intellectually disabled and dependent on others for his cares, how in Korea, so much of life is literally guided by the seasons and how our weakened planet's climate may erase centuries of this culture. The raw emotions spilling out of the essay needed some repair and care from loving, literary editorial eyes.

The destructive onward march of capitalism, even into the "independent" literary space, where Catapult Magazine can just cease in a day because the climate change heiress wants to pivot to "wellness" (for whom?) seems depressingly unstoppable. Which is why I am so grateful for this journal that centers activist voices of writer of color and will continue to bravely "cast lines between the future and the past, the possible and the impossible."

Originally published in July 2017 online at asterixjournal.com

Firelei Báez on Generosity and Freedom in Art

Angie Cruz and Firelei Báez

I met Firelei Báez at The Andy Warhol Museum for over an hour. She was taking a short break from installing her one-woman show Firelei Báez: Bloodlines. That day, high school students had been recruited to help her paint the walls, built especially for the show. Jessica Beck, the curator, had been painting alongside Firelei. The spirit and energy around the show reminded me of my Dominican family back home, when something had to get done, everyone rolled their sleeves and just got to work. The following is our conversation.

Angie Cruz: I'm thrilled that you currently have a solo show at The Warhol. I have been thinking a lot about the invisibility of Latino/a artists in mainstream media and it's exciting for Pittsburgh, and for me , as a Dominicana, to have you here. In an interview you said that you've had the experience of being the first Latina/o or Caribbean artist to present in a museum. Why do you think that is, in 2017?

Firelei Báez: Latino and Caribbean artists have been working within mainstream American institutions all through history. Take Gordon Matta Clark, who was of Chilean descent but is solely cited as an American Artist. It is through the efforts of courageous academics and artists within the last thirty years that artists like me can proudly claim our Caribbean seat at the table. I am the first Caribbeña artist to have a solo show at The Warhol Museum.

AC: You once said that if you went way back, you'd cite Leonardo da Vinci as an influence. But recently , you cited Felix Gonzalez-Torres and Ana Mendieta as influences.

FB: We have such a broad lexicon to look onto. Da Vinci's book of drawings was the first art book I ever saw and that was in my sophomore year of high school. I love Julie Mehretu's work, and although there are amazing male artists, I make an effort to focus on women artists who are canonical and who have shifted my idea of art. For me they are Lorna Simpson and Julie Mehretu. I love the work of Kara Walker, Wangechi Mutu and Simone Leigh. Also writers like Arundhati Roy, Zadie Smith and Julia Alvarez.

AC: What's interesting about many of the artists you mentioned is that they identify as African-American artists. So for you as a Dominican—
FB: In the U.S., the younger generation of Dominican artists are more informed by African American art. Many of the Dominican artists in D.R. who were successful, moved to Paris, they looked to Europe and came from a certain class. So as a Dominican raised in the U.S. but who spent her formative years in the D. R., I didn't grow up with any concept of art. It was through public schooling and after-school programs in the U.S. that I realized art is something that people do. I made art all the time–my family is creative and I would make paper dolls for the neighborhood– the act of making was always with me, but the idea of becoming an artist, I didn't have that in D.R.

AC: This was also true for me as a writer. I was informed by writers like Baldwin and Morrison. When I read them I was like, this is my story too.

FB: Yeah it's the parallel. Our story is so complex that you have to have a filter. Discourse in the U.S. is–black or white–there isn't the multivalence you'd have in Latin America. I think it comes in part out of religion. Catholicism allows for all these different threads, syncretism. You can't have images in Protestant religions for instance, so you need very clear ideas of what is and can't be. Have you seen casta paintings from Latin America?

AC: No, I haven't.

FB: They're paintings that told their owners who they were to society based on race. They existed within the Catholic religion and were displayed near the home's altar, with the saints that were meant to be prayed to on a daily basis. In these spaces, people were encouraged to mix, with this goal of mestizaje. They were supposed to enact this social violence. At the same time there are some of the first intimate, and tender portraits of mixed families.

AC: I'm so happy you're saying this about Protestantism versus Catholic aesthetics, because when I teach books by people of color in particular, some students will say, it's interesting but I just don't feel it? And I understand how they feel because that's how I feel about certain writing in the U.S. that is often celebrated. For years I have been thinking about how our spiritual formation informs our aesthetic leaning and consumption of culture. As a younger writer in the MFA workshop I was told my work had too many characters, too much drama. But I need more drama. When I see your visual work I understand a Dominicaness in it. There's this rich, multi-sensory provocation. I feel it.

FB: Thank you. They don't know how much restraint we need to have to show a fraction of our experiences. There is so much more to say and this is just the needle's eye being allowed at this moment. We as immigrants have access to all this information, all these rich complex histories which we have no problem understanding and translating because we're used to seeing ourselves as Other, and Other in ourselves. AC: I feel like there's definitely a lot of momentum for African American art and literature right now in the U.S.. How do you feel about the reception for works from the Spanish-speaking Caribbean?

FB: It's funny, I'm a Dominican citizen, but I was raised here in the U.S.. My work addresses race and class. In D.R. they would be like, what's wrong with your brain? Why are you speaking about these issues? I exist as a bridge. In this in-between space. Right now, I'm either Latin American or I'm American. The art collections are built around those two identity politics. So someone like me has to choose a camp. There's no space for that in-between.

AC: The borderland.

FB: Exactly. With the Latinx movement, it's the idea of valuing that space, of making it a valid voice with concrete weight. But right now I either have to be Latin American or Black. If I show too much at Studio Museum in Harlem then El Museo del Barrio resents it.

AC: Really?

FB: I've experienced that. They'll be like, oh she's all Black now. Oh no, she's all Latina. You can't be enough of this or enough of that. The African diaspora is bigger than the United States. Take Brazil or Martinique. That tiny Caribbean island had more African slaves brought there than the entirety of the U.S. before the Louisiana Purchase. We in the African diaspora share similar experiences, to a greater degree outside the United States. Conversations around race in the U.S. are so didactic. This in part drove, in my opinion, the clarity of the discourse and policies of the Civil Rights movement. In romance language-speaking spaces, like Brazil and Latin America, race is always addressed in terms of mestizaje, supposedly never prizing one race over the other, but in all honesty pushing for a more European ending.

AC: What about U.S. Latino/a art? Where does it fit?

FB: What's held as the canon of Latin American art is European modernism. In every sphere, you're following this European model, and the people who are showing in that are of a certain class. There's Carmen Herrera for instance, a Cuban woman artist who got her first Whitney biennial at almost a hundred years old. She went to Paris in her twenties, and spent most of her life in the U.S. Anyone reading through this would be like, she's Latinx, she's a Latina, she's Cuban-born but spent most of her life here in the U.S.. She is being positioned within high modernism in Brazil. With artists like Lygia Clark and Hélio Oiticica. That's how they find value in her work. There was latino/a work being done even before the WPA, and hopefully that work will be written about differently.

AC: In the book industry many people collapse latino/a and latin American books in the same lists. Oftentimes the books are translations. It can create less visibility to the dearth of U.S. Latino/a narratives. It fuels the idea that we are foreigners. Don't you think?

FB: In a recent news cast there was a segment on immigration. During the caller segment a man asked "how are they vetting Puerto Ricans?" And the person taking the calls was like, you do realize they're American citizens? We don't prevent someone from Iowa coming to the main city, or someone from Hawaii from coming here. But this idea, because there's a different language being spoken perhaps, that you don't belong, or you're something that should be filtered out, is heartbreaking.

AC: So you grew up in Dajabon which is the border city between Dominican Republic and Haiti, loaded with a troubling history and also now very contentious. How has growing up in a space where there is a stark difference between the lush green environment of the Dominican Republic and then the deforested landscape of Haiti, has informed your work?

FB: Ok, so think of the French Enlightenment, the Empire, Parisian opulence: the money that fueled all of that was coming out of indigo and sugar from the colony of Saint- Domingue and Martinique. So that lush landscape we have in DR, that fertile soil, is all in Haiti as well. They were still paying billions of dollars in debt to France into the twentieth century for their independence. When Trujillo was doing the Massacre, they [Haiti] were still paying a huge embargo for their independence. I didn't even know this until I was doing research on the palace of Sans Souci, near Cap Haitian. Dominican Republic paid a similar independence debt to Spain as well but while still being part of a global commerce. It's incredible. Not only do you have this war, but to get back into world trade, you have to pay monetarily for your freedom.

AC: One of your works that I find provocative is the Paper Bag Test, for example. I love how the eyes come in—they cross the border of the Paper Bag Test. It's very haunting to look at the work.

FB: I wanted the viewer to come to terms with there being a human being behind all that.

AC: Skin comes up a lot in your work, projections of nature and the outside onto the skin. Why skin?

FB: It's not so much about skin itself but rather ideas around the body. Or ideas around what forms how we treat land and body. This is how I position the figure in my work. If a figure is in a white ground, isolated on a picture, on a plane, it's referencing things like Carl Linnaeus's taxonomy. Which was first developed as a way for humans to 'factually' tally the living beings and plants around them; but instead allowed for horrible things to be done to people and nature outside of Europe. The Dutch believe there were cannibals and vampires along with beavers and moose in the new world for instance. It's more of the body as a specimen that can be explored in order to reveal something of the viewer in the process. Any of my Ciguapa paintings are an example of this. They are physical, heavy seeming figures that fuse with landscape. If the figure has a ground, then it is more about creating this space that diffuses the weight of the body. The surrounding color voids physicality and gets closer to spirit, to a psychological interiority. These near abstractions act like Rorschach's where the viewer projects themselves onto the picture. It is perhaps more freeing and intimate for me in the studio.

AC: Historically, skin has always been like the container, the separation from the outside world, but now we understand that skin is the communicator, the interface. Even the way we think about skin has changed so much. Also, thinking about communicating the projection, not just of other people but of nature, and in some ways it gives agency to nature.

FB: I agree. When I was a kid I was told to control how I shed my hair, it seemed strange because it's melding European witchcraft or voodoo, East and West. Every part of your physical self is tied to your spirit. So one warning was if my hair was taken by a bird, I'd be stuck in limbo, because they exist between heaven and earth. You'd lose control of your body.

AC: I love that.

FB: As a little girl, I was taught to be beholden to nature. To think of it as something with immense power that can control you. But coming to the States, birds are grooming princesses on TV, humans are masters of their environment. Coming from the Dominican Republic I was like 'listen girl, you're in danger!', your body and your soul are tied together, and if anything takes it, your control is gone.

AC: So you were in Miami when you decided to go to Cooper Union. Your family was good with that decision?

FB: They never were. They're coming to terms with it now because I'm doing things.

AC: You're very successful!

FB: But even now they're just like, ok maybe. They're like: you need health insurance, a husband, kids, a home, this car, and then we'll see if you're successful.

AC: So what do you think about this precarious moment for artists? Trump threats to cut NEA funding but also we're in a hyper-professionalized moment.Angela Davis said our imaginations have been privatized, right? What does that do to art?

FB: As a child of an immigrant, I knew to juggle several balls at the same time. When I was in college I had five jobs sometimes. I can do anything.

AC: But what do you think the role of artists and writers is right now?

FB: Well, because art is being hyper-professionalized, it can create rigidity in how you respond. We deserve to have quality of life, and that's the biggest push toward professionalizing. If you are working for someone you shouldn't do it for free. But at the same time, there's more people working for free for institutions. Or art is being used as a Band-Aid to help the things that social policy isn't working on.

AC: I have seen some of my favorite museums move toward edutainment. I worked as a teaching artist at museums for years. It was a great gig but why are artists dropping into schools for a day? Schools should be creating dynamic curriculum where art is prioritized.

FB: Often art programs directed to black and brown kids are geared to improve their health, to prevent crimes, to make them not get pregnant. It's never about art for itself and expressing their creativity. Art can help you break out of that confine.

AC: So in this moment, you're not terribly terrified for yourself or the world?

FB: We're in the beginning of a dark age. What are we gonna do? When I was growing up we'd spend summers with my grandmother and aunt who were Seventh Day Adventists, and for them, at the turn of the 20th century they believed the world was gonna end! They've all been on rapture-wait mode for the past hundred years. Though I have not been religious since I was twelve, that is still the mindset: be ready.

AC: For you, what were some of the main challenges as an artist?

FB: Not knowing where your income is going to be. Having to move often. I went to a different school every year since I was in the first grade. I've just been ready for whatever comes. Not being afraid of hard work. Which is a mindset you have to get out of because working helps you survive but in order to thrive you have to move beyond survival. To believe you belong in this space.

AC: Do you remember that moment?

FB: I don't think I'm there yet. I probably need five more years of feedback to feel like, ok, what's next?

AC: Who is your ideal audience? And who do you think you're seeking feedback from?

FB: I make work for my mom and my sisters. For people who share a similar history to mine. And if that history happens to strike a chord in someone who has a different experience, then that's great. I'm always shocked and happy when I've shown work in Utah and Nevada, and there's excitement. The histories I'm introducing to them are not familiar, not even to Dominicans themselves. If you give enough of a roadmap people might be excited to read more on it. A woman of color is usually in my ideal audience.

AC: But if I look at your work without knowing the history, I would think, I love the way that body is moving. Or I'll be curious about why there's something happening in a certain way. How do you communicate through beauty?

FB: There's a visual seduction that happens, and then the sting, if you are generous enough to keep looking. I'm asking a lot of the viewer. I want them to meet me at a halfway point. I'll give enough for the viewer to start creating the narrative. People come with their own histories. Especially if you're from another country. Folklore is a place that has so much overlap globally because we go through similar experiences. So when I'm talking about a Ciguapa from Hispaniola, there's a trickster figure that's similar to it in Brazil, India or Ghana.

AC: If you had the ear of Trump for two minutes and you asked him to look at three works—

FB: I would do this: I would take a course in hypnotism, I would try to hypnotize him, the visuals could be anything, a Rauschenberg for instance.

AC: Are there any things that you think would help him see?

FB: To have his body be our body. The reason he doesn't see is because he doesn't need to see. His body, his children, the things he cares about are protected. I would hypnotize him and say , "You are a woman of color."

AC: But what about works that you have found incredibly transformational to yourself? Or have helped you re-see something? Could you name a work?

FB: Lorna Simpson's, Seven Day Weather Forecast. Oor Kara Walker's Diorama Gone: An Historical Romance. Or Goya's, Terrors. Or the mural of the buddha at the Met–like going to a temple and seeing the human intent behind them. You see this reach for something beyond the body, beyond our present existence. Agnes Martin's rooms that are like chapels, you know? It's like this reach towards spirit, always. They're anchored in physical space but there's always a reach for something greater. But I don't think any of these ephemeral things would work with Trump.

AC: So my other question is—and I didn't even ask you what you're planning to work on for this show, which I need to ask you because it's important! But before that, what are some young artists that you're excited to see kind of blow up, that you want to namedrop right now?

FB: I'm working with some of them in this show in Ukraine. Dineo Seshee Bopape, Phoebe Boswell and Martine Syms do incredible work. And Kenny Rivero is a Dominicano around my age who makes the most sublime paintings.

AC: So what are you working on here at the Warhol?

FB: So here, we're basically continuing the premise of the Perez Exhibition—Bloodlines. Which formally traced social movements within the black diaspora in the entirety of the New World. Seeing how actions in North America, like the Harlem Renaissance or the Black Power Movement were all in conversation with movements that were happening in the Caribbean. And even if you think of North African revolutions, they were also being informed by Caribbean theory. So making concrete and obvious those interactions, down to a formal level, connecting the black power fist, the socialist fist with the figa or el azabache. At the same time as the Perez Museum of Art in Miami show there was a sister exhibition at the Utah Museum of Contemporary Art that was titled Patterns of Resistance, and this exhibition at The Warhol will be a a melding of those two.

*The show was at The Andy Warhol Museum until May 21, 2017. **Firelei Báez: Bloodlines** was organized by Pérez Art Museum Miami Assistant Curator María Elena Ortiz. The Pittsburgh presentation was coordinated by Jessica Beck, The Warhol's associate curator of art.*

-

Editors' Note: this interview has been condensed and edited for clarity. The original conversation is available to read online in full along with corresponding images from the exhibit.

Originally published in January 2017 online at asterixjournal.com

---

Reparations

Rosamond S. King

see   through   people!

on sale today!

35 year old   boys   and girls

breeding boys

        to lighten your race

breeding girls

       for fun and profit

backs bent every morning

legs open every night

see   through   people!

cheap!

Originally published in our Fall 2017 issue, *Dirty Laundry*

This Moment of Mine/ Este Momento Mío

Marigloria Palma,

translated by Carina del Valle Schorske

I drink down my aspirins and watch the stars shiver.
This is my time, time of jet planes and plastic bombs.
Atomic era of the calculator. Ecological time,
biochemical time, transplant time, cancer time.

In a corner of the sky the tainted moon
(prostitute moon) puts her rabbits out to pasture
over her beaten breast. She passes, meditative, dragging
her swarm of wilted lilies, her dusty bitter God-help-you.

Man defiled her with his ideas (his scientific alchemy)
blasting rockets between her radiant hips and storming
her secret locks. Then he climbed up and spat in her face,
digging his heels in her chest. Brutalized moon

without mystery or shadow. Man has stripped you down
with his hands of clay. He's blackened you with his magic
machine of flame-for-brains. He's crushed your thighs
of foam and cream, your throat of milk, your transparent pubis.

But still you laugh, impassive, lifting your brow like a mad queen
on the eve of a coup… On earth the poet thinks of you and sobs:
don of words, genius of fine-wired syllables, he fashions you
a clever new snatch of blood and torment: a poem, sky-blue.

Este Momento Mío (de La noche y otras flores eléctricas)

Trago aspirinas y miro las estrellas parpadear.
Este es mi tiempo, tiempo de avión a chorro
y bomba plastic. Era de la calculadora
y fuerza atomica.
Tiempo de ecologia, de transplantes,
de cáncer y bioquimica.

Por un rincón del cielo la luna mancillada
(luna prostituida) pastorea sus conejos
con los senos vencidos. Pasa meditativa
arrastrando el enjambre de sus lirios ajados
y el Diostesalve polvoriento y ácido.

El hombre la ultrajó con sus ideas
(su cientifica alquimia) disparando cohetes
que ensuciaron sus radiantes caderas
y desentrorinzaron sus secretos invictos.
Despues subió hasta ella y le escupió la cara
Hundiéndole en el pecho los tacones.

Luna brutalizada sin misterio ni sombra.
Te ha desnudado el hombre con sus manos de arcilla.
Te ha mancillado el hombre con la maquina magica
De su ardiente cerebro. Ha estrujado tus muslos
De natilla espumosa, tu garganta de leche,
Tu transparente pubis.

Pero aun rielas impavida levantando la grente
Como una reina loca depronto destronada…
En la tierra el poeta te contempla y solloza
Y con don de palabras y alambritos de silabas
Te fabrica ingenioso una nueva vagina
Con su angustia y su sangre: un celeste poema.

Originally published in our Fall 2016 issue, *What We Love*

On Eschatological Radio Angels Flying In The Troposphere

Karen An-Hwei Lee

Millennial engineers of faltering air, not eschatological radio angels tighten struts, bolts, and cantilevers of eternal design. Angels guard antique equipment, invented in principle by our original architect, logophile, and alpha-omega *abba*.

Shoulders of unseeded rain encircle the troposphere,
　　sweet jaggery of ferns.

Northern lights, the auroras, riff magnetic jazz above the poles.
　　A low-frequency hum
　　　　　　　　signals human civilization or vice versa—

The long winter salts a tangible road of devotion. *Please tune in.*
Do you hear me? Radio angels neither hunger nor thirst: *Tune in.*
Desiderata of violent coronal flares, gore-jewels of salvation.

No one sees who is there —lights on
　　　　　　　　hovering afield.

Karen An-Hwei Lee on "On Eschatological Radio Angels Flying In The Troposphere"

What inspired this piece?

My father is a retired aerospace engineer, so my imagination was edified by flight since I was a girl when he taught me how to fold paper airplanes. In this poem, flight takes on a metaphysical valence with the otherworldly image of "radio angels" and "gore-jewels of salvation."

Originally published in our Summer 2017 issue,
Kitchen Table Translation

Chance Encounter/
Lo Casual

Cecilia Vicuña translated by Rosa Alcalá

The idea of coming upon the unexpected
as something carefully arranged
by a prior hand that linked
all its forms aesthetically
to explain a disordered garden
at the height of its disorder,
a gesture not yet carried out, gently stirring
with no way of knowing what will become of it.

Indeterminacy, the musical
sway of certain grasses
left to fend for themselves
brown and parched
consequence of an emotion
the owner suffered
she who so lovingly tended
to the wallflowers
and now has let them
grow wild
who visits the garden
only to let it languish.
Precarious, given to its fate,

all has become weary
and by chance lives.

29 August 1970

Lo Casual
La idea de encontrar lo casual como algo
que estaba cuidadosamente preparado
por una mano anterior que encadenó
sus formas estéticamente
para explicar un jardín desordenado
que está en el punto preciso de su desorden,
un gesto sin consumar, que se agita levemente
sin que se sepa qué va a ser de él.

La indeterminación, la musicalidad
del movimiento de algunas hierbas
abandonadas a sí mismas
doradas de sequedad
a causa de una emoción
que sufrió su dueña
que antes se ocupaba
tan tiernamente del alelí
y ahora ha dejado
que todo crezca
y solo visita el jardín
para dejarlo languidecer.
Azaroso y muelle
todo se ha cansado
y vive por casualidad.

29 agosto 1970

Originally published in May 2018 online at asterixjournal.com

Topping from the Bottom: A Conversation with Kegels for Hegel and Patricia Montoya

Amy Sara Carroll

In bone-crushing times, don't mourn, organize.
And, reach for a torch song.
Or two.

For years I've been a groupie of the conceptual art project making queer love songs to philosophers called Kegels for Hegel (K4H). It's consequently my pleasure to do this flash interview with them for Aster(ix). *To make an ideal situation even better, I'm thrilled that Patricia Montoya—a recent collaborator with K4H whose video/film installations have equally mesmerized me—was willing to join the conversation.*

Spoiler alert: speaking of longitudinal queer influence and kinship, many thanks to Angie Cruz for soliciting this piece for Aster(ix). *Exercise your kegels! Lean into our exchange below.*

AMY: Describe the delectable project of Kegels for Hegel (K4H). Possibly begin by detailing K4H's ecstasy of influence, or, more specifically, by offering an account of the band's humorous name as it relates to *I Wanna Fight You to the Death (Love Song to G.W.F. Hegel).*

K4H: We were graduate students in 2010 when we created Kegels for Hegel and wrote our first song to German philosopher G.W.F. Hegel.

One of us had a pretty memorable orgasm while reading Hegel, but it wasn't inspired by anything hot about Hegel—it was really just a way to try to stay awake while reading hours upon hours of dense social theory.

At the time we wrote our first song and created a name for the project, we were living in a rat-infested dirty hippie co-op in Rochester, New York. We became kegel evangelists once we learned that it's possible for one's organs to fall out of one's vagina (Prolapse! It's real! Google it!). There's a profoundly practical component to this project! Another practicality: Our kegel within was awakened as a conceptual art project, and we started synthesizing interdisciplinarity with our super smart friends, composing most of our songs with GarageBand, making music videos, and performing the work live.

AMY: Come again, can you go into greater detail about K4H as a conceptual project? There are many debates in contemporary poetry about the merits of conceptual writing. For some time, I have been thinking and writing about ways of reframing and reclaiming the conceptual. Selfishly then I'd love to hear you expand on your ideas about the conceptual.

K4H: Knowledge is often described as penetrative and ideas as seminal. We wanted the project to consider knowledge or inquiry from the other end of the penetration metaphor: the grabbing onto something and making it a part of you. We wrote an invagination manifesto about it...It's worth invaginating this interview with it, too. And, of course, vaginas do this, but we are definitely not into reproducing this idea that vagina = woman. Everyone has an anus, and anal kegels are possible, too! We were also thinking about re-framing classic models of power and penetration, considering the potential of "topping from the bottom," or thinking of grabbing onto things as an active act, à la filmmaker and theorist Nguyen Tan Hoang's *Bottomhood is Powerful,* and musicians Lady's "Yankin" and Fly Young Red's "Throw that Boy Pussy."

AMY: I suppose that my prior questions implicitly have wondered about the following, but now I want to explicitly ask: How does this collaboration intersect—or not—with other aspects of your solo and shared life/work? In particular, I am interested in your "day jobs" as art historian-curator and anthropologist and the way that K4H challenges "prudish" boundaries maintained between the critical and the creative.

K4H: We are a collective that works with anyone who wants to join us, and those people are often academics. We have had anthropologists and art historians, among other colleagues and friends, as collaborators. And as academics, the founders of K4H, and some of our collaborators, are semi-anonymous for a few reasons. Some of those reasons have to do with the way we wanted to foreground collaboration. But another key reason is that several people involved in the project are in precarious situations in relation to their day jobs in the academic and museum worlds. And what you mention about the prudish boundaries between the critical and the creative is one reason they are hesitant to come out. Another reason is the raunchy, sexually-explicit nature of our work. As far as the founders go, one of us kept K4H a secret from most colleagues for the first few years but has increasingly given fewer fucks and is now totally out about it. The other is still more careful at this particular moment. During our worst moments of anxiety, we both imagined some kind of a prudish cis het white dude dean googling our names before signing off on something having to do with a hire or tenure or something and then being like, "NOT THAT DIRTY SLUT!"

AMY: Yes, sadly such a scenario is very plausible and sounds all too familiar to me. I'm so glad you're finding ways to navigate these hazards in your life/work juggling acts. But, let's not give those cis het whites dude deans any more time in our interview. I'd like to shift gears to travel further into the realms of institutional critique. Returning to the flesh and the flash: for now and in perpetuity, what does "Love" have to do with all of the above?

K4H: Love comes into play in the collaborative aspect of the project. We are always trying to imagine forms of connection that are alternatives to the hetero-monogamous nuclear family structure. For our *Pastelegram* issue we created a queer kinship chart that was inspired by both the kinds of kinship charts that anthropologist make and the chart made on *The L Word* showing who all of the queer women were fucking. We are also thinking of Tim Dean's reading of men giving each other HIV as a form of creating kinship. We will probably not have children, but we think of our K4H collaborations as a way of generating new things and creating queer kinship through playing/working with our friends and colleagues and lovers and crushes and mentors.

AMY: Okay, I'm hooked. I absolutely love this! I also have to confess that I've been obsessed with drawing queer kinship diagrams in part because I do have a child and I need for him to know that myriad alternatives of connection exist. I take seriously Eve Kosofsky Sedgwick's "How to Bring Your Kids up Gay"! To that end, I think I need your help drawing a diagram for an essay I'm currently completing on the work of Jesusa Rodríguez and Liliana Felipe. And, following that tangent: all this reminds me that I believe that the first time I met one of you we later went to see an evening of cabaret at El Vicio, formerly El Hábito, in Mexico City. Rodríguez and Felipe's work has been amazing in its reclamation of the cabaret genre and it's hugely impacted my own thinking, writing, and artmaking. Could we collaborate on a song for them one day in the near future? Pivot: staying on track, can you talk more about your own past, current, and future género-bending torch songs?

K4H: Oooooh, yes, we should absolutely collaborate on a song for Rodríguez and Felipe! Like you wrote, Amy, torch songs — sentimental songs about unrequited love— these were what we thought of as our genre. We were originally thinking of the banality of most love songs and wanting to make them more ambivalent to reflect our strange feelings about being shaped by these white Western philosophers whom we felt inspired by and interested in yet also had gripes with and felt we needed to talk back to. But we were also influenced by the genre of the *narcocorrido.* The narco ballader writes songs to people, often to larger than life anti-heroes. So our love songs hit somewhere in the range of ambivalence. And the songs also became about an ambivalence toward philosophy with its dead white dude canon upholding the archetype of the Real Philosopher. So we have used the project to write love songs to thinkers who we believe should be considered philosophers, too.

We call them love songs, but most of them can probably be more accurately characterized as lust songs! Thinking of them as lust songs perhaps makes more sense in that there's something about getting turned on by ideas.

Amy, you actually wrote a love song of sorts to José Muñoz as part of the *Pastelegram* project. Well, actually it was a poem, and we were supposed to put it to music, but we loved the way it sounded and never found the right music to add to it. Could you tell us a bit about that poem in relation to love and queer kinship?

AMY: Hmmm.… Thanks for indulging me here and validating my tendencies toward the tangential. Long live the flipped script–talk about queering genres! For starters, I'm absolutely honored to be on your queer kinship chart. I wrote the poem that you included in *Pastelegram* spontaneously on the afternoon it details. As I wrote it, I was thinking about how Muñoz writes about the ordinariness of queerness in the Frank O'Hara poem, "Having a Coke With You," but also about what I can only read as Muñoz's prose poem, his compact provocation on queer methexis (note the "me" and the "mex" versus the "methe," "x," and the "is" rising to the surface in this curious word), published under the title "Toward a Methexic Queer Media" in *GLQ*. I also was thinking about the brilliant poet-scholar Fred Moten's collection *B Jenkins* (bearing the name of his mother) wherein he wrote poems to and about people in his life centrally or peripherally–another queer kinship chart, to be sure.

Mostly, however, I was trying to work through a mourning that I wasn't entitled to claim. I had met, but did not know, José Muñoz. Still, as a graduate student, I was deeply impacted by his book *Disidentifications*. I frequently tell that story to students in the seminars I now teach like this: In undergraduate school, I first read Anzaldúa's *Borderlands/La Frontera*. The book was so important to me, I couldn't leave my dorm room without it. I carried it everywhere like a talisman, or better put, like a tailswoman. In graduate school, *Disidentifications* had a comparable visceral affect on me. I remember a dear friend and I spending so many joyful hours loving *Disidentifications*. We treated it something like *the* lustful torch song of our generation. We staged engagements with it in a performance workshop that we took with the incomparable Holly Hughes. We swooned over it in an art history class with the equally incomparable Kristine Stiles. It became our touchstone and deep point of connection… and, so I shamelessly loop back to queer kinship and love!

PATRICIA: José Muñoz is a great influence in my development as artist, very supportive of the work I made in NYC in the 90s through a paper that the cultural critic, Berta Jottar wrote on my piece "El Culebrero, la muerte de un Colombiano y el acordeonista que no esta" (1996). José made artmaking sound possible, part of everyday life for the wandering soul I was in NYC in those days.

I've pursued a career where love and work are interchangeable in the way that love, in fact, is the work

ONE MEMBER OF K4H: Ugh, love. I just recently realized that the academic book I'm in the middle of revising is actually about love, which it wasn't supposed to be, originally. So I'm currently dealing with my own anxieties about saying something smart about love that's connected to the smart things other people have said about love. In my academic work, I'm thinking through love as non-sovereignty, love as obligation, and love relationships as entailing both coercion and support. But I'm writing about the love between sex workers, their families, their pimps, and the missionaries who hope to turn them into former sex workers, so my approach to love is grounded in those complicated relationships.

AMY: I can't wait to read what you write. I know you won't revert to the missionary position in your scholarly speculations. Keep on Kegeling across your practice! If you want to tell us more about this, please do; or, shifting gears again, can you reflect on on K4H as a queer Latin/x American intervention/durational performance?

K4H: Most of our songs and music videos engage some of the ideas of the thinkers we write about in a way that sexualizes them–and also ourselves–and makes reference to non-normative sex acts. One of us writes about the whore stigma, which is used to discipline all women but is most violently deployed against sex workers, racially marked people, poor people and gender non-conforming people. Some of our songs invoke conquest scripts in ways that invoke ideas about race, gender, and power. Jillian Hernandez, our friend and collaborator, developed the concept of raunch aesthetics to refer to cultural production that engages explicit sexuality and humor for the pleasures of minority audiences, especially queers and POC, who are often seen as sexually excessive or freaky. This is something we were always doing on a more instinctual or visceral level, but now we've got a concept for it, which is cool. We need to write a love/lust song to Jill. *Queridx reader, please consider collaborating with us on this!*

AMY: Speaking of collaboration, you've said so much already about the latter as act and concept, I hope you will forgive me for trying to pin you down on one collaboration in particular. Could we talk more specifically about the impetus behind your Valentine's Day 2018 music video *Take Me to Yr Borderlands (Canción de amor a Gloria E. Anzaldúa)*? I suppose I could reframe this to also address another of my repetition compulsions in this interview, too. Broken record: what does "Love" code-switching into "amor" have to do with all of this? Also, Patricia, would you join us again?

K4H: Regarding Conquest scripts, we wrote the Spanish hook on after a disturbing trip to the Border Patrol Museum in El Paso, Texas while thinking about colonization, neocolonialism, and the militarization of the US/Mexico Border.

> Te quiero conquistar
> Como las Americas
> Te quiero saborear
> Como un elote
> Y vas a trabajar

No hay beneficios
Y te va a gustar

We were then trying to come up with a philosopher to dedicate this to, but we couldn't find someone we hated enough, so we dedicated it to the makers of the Arizona bill to ban ethnic studies, made a 1 minute video, and called it "Aztlán." Like yeah, motherfuckers, you're afraid that if we teach young people history, they will rise up and plan a reconquista? Fine, let's do it.

But then we had the idea to re-frame it as dyke power play and to write it as a love song to dyke chicana feminist Gloria Anzaldúa. We titled it to honor her transgressions of linguistic borderlands, her code-switching.

AMY: I am fascinated by your careful recounting of the transformation of this song! And, the changes continue! Patricia, would you also be willing to answer question #2 as it relates to your past and future work as a video/film/installation artist? Or, perhaps you're interesting in reflecting (more) on "queer methexic media"?

PATRICIA: My collaboration with K4H started when I saw their videos for the first time and was presented with the 30 sec teaser for the Gloria Anazaldúa music video that was shot in Mexico City My aesthetics and sensibility are very different from K4H's and I wasn't sure if I could match the electricity of their videos and the song itself.

K4H: Well, you pulled it off!

AMY: Tell us more! Can you describe in greater detail your aesthetics? One of my favorite things about collaboration is the ways that the process transforms everyone involved. My own aesthetic has shifted dramatically and continues to do so via collaboration, itself a vehicle of invagination. Does this explain why so many of our academic (especially in the humanities) and artistic "parents" warn against producing collaborative work?

PATRICIA: I'm rather a slow, old school, Pablo Neruda, Dulce Maria Loynaz, kind of poet; but as a documentarian, my experimental videos are absurdist theater adaptations. I was excited to collaborate in a project with K4H's contemporary, queer and trans youth of color aesthetic. But in a generous, curious, open spirit, both K4H's and my own, I offered footage I had shot in Tijuana from previous projects. They intervened with their vast research, imagination and enthusiasm, and we joined forces.

The three of us teach at universities and made the video during academic breaks, which prolonged the process more than we had anticipated. Also, I struggled to deliver what I could to the project, a contribution that was original to me. But this is the creative process, as I understand it, anyway.

AMY: Patricia, can we hear more about how you understand the creative process? One of my favorite moments in this music video is when you "float" through it, levitating to the tune. In particular, I love how you are horizontal, yet still in motion in that sequence. It becomes a sly signature, a signaling of your presence in the project, but is "understated" in comparison to K4H's delightfully excessive presencing. How does your position as such relate to your current project addressing the legacies/ghosts of Gloria Anzaldúa? And/or, do you consider yourself to be a border filmmaker?

I've written about post-1980s border undocumentaries, many originating in the Tijuana-San Diego corridor at the close of my recent book *REMEX: Toward an Art History of the NAFTA Era*. It's the portion of the book which feels the most unfinished and hurried to me, which is ironic because a goodly number of the films I consider are indebted to slow or art cinema. I know you received your MFA from the University of California, San Diego. Can you talk about that department's and region's lasting influences on your work? Finally, per my tired recourse to the cut and the loop: I'd welcome any insights you have re: amor (vs. everything).

PATRICIA: I am exploring the documentary and the essay film and experimental cinema in relation to music video production and imagining ways to cross pollinate these genres in future pieces.

Regarding my love for Gloria Anzaldúa in my work, making the video enabled me to play with and confront my own ghostly haunting. The lingering presence of my uptight Catholic upbringing began to disperse as we followed Anzaldúa's borderlands theories, as we composed together a polyamorously sexual, raunchy, and anti-purist aesthetics. The creative process afforded unexpected convergences and coincidences. We filmed the video in Houston, Texas, although we had hoped to film it in Anzaldúa's hometown. My love for the cities of Houston and Tijuana as places of inspiration, history and connectivity informed the work. My family is from Colombia, and an entire portion of my extended family moved to Houston in the 80s and calls it home. My grandmother is buried in Houston. I had spent a great deal of time in San Diego and Tijuana, but filming with K4H in Houston helped to make the Texas link to the borderlands real to me. I had visited periodically ever since the 1980s but did not know the city in the ways that K4H presented it to me.

My experience at UCSD was life defining. The many good memories of my time there are still vivid; the friendships still strong. Looking back, I realize that we were supposed to learn how to be artists in the Visual Arts program. I did not know that at the time, though. Only now, after I've had a few detours, do I see how invaluable that lesson is. I guess the essence of things is in the obvious.

AMY: In a scent or taste that lingers…

PATRICIA: Regarding the lingering effects of life experiences, I would say that the connection between political artwork, education, identity formation, the constant process of becoming, the recurring themes in my work such as the fluidity of borders and urban landscapes, are tied to my desire to live fully, to be open more than ever to intellectual curiosity and experiences, to new challenges and transformations. These are the spiritual ruminations that connect me to Gloria Anzaldúa's work and the gift I was given by collaborating with K4H.

K4H: Patricia, we had fun introducing you to our strange Texican spicy and sweet snacks. The video features many shots of Texican and Northern Mexican treats like chamoyadas, Flamin' Hot Cheetos® smothered in nacho cheese and jalapeños, and pickle juice snow cones. We don't know if Anzaldúa consumed these kinds of snacks, but making this visual reference to the culinary borderlands was important to us.

AMY: Yum! *Note to the reader: it might be best to view the videos and read this interview over again while snacking on the aforementioned.* I never expected this conversation to turn on and return to Texas! I'm from Corpus Christi originally, somewhere in between Houston and Anzaldúa's birth/burial grounds. Patricia, I love that you are pushing us to connect kinship charts and maps. Again, do you think of yourself as a border artist? K4H, could you chime in to respond to the same question? *Note to the reader: I definitely identify as a borderlands writer. Previously, I asked about a queer Latin/x American aesthetic, but could/ should we get* both *more specific and more general to accent queer borderlands' praxes? It might make for a nice open end for and to our conversation.*

PATRICIA: Yes, I do consider myself a border artist. I found myself at the Mexico-US border. I loved being able to cross back and forth from "the end of the USA and the beginning of Latin America," as my former professor at UCSD, Teddy Cruz, would say of the fence traversing the beach into the ocean in Playas de Tijuana. *No olvido lo que sentí al verme mirando el continente entero desde el cerco*, right there and then my work found its place, its purpose. I love that fence because it is a reminder of the ugly, painful, and horrific in US imperialism and of Latin America's defiance and fight for freedom embedded in its culture. I'm developing project ideas that will take me back to San Diego/TJ. More on that, I hope, soon.

K4H: Yes, we both identify as borderlands artists, among other things. The space of the hyphen, or that phrase that Word® underlines as a spelling error because it doesn't know it to exist; those theoretical space of signification and resignification seem like home– places of creation, of dissent, of resistance because their meanings are still being defined or we haven't yet made words to define them. We both ended up pursuing academic projects that had to do with the US/Mexico relationship—one of us in a Mexican border city and the other in Mexico City. So as a grounded response, yes, we grew up in Texas and California, as well as bouncing around between Mexico and Anglo-Europe, in families where the borders between Mexican and White infused the way that we learned about the world.

Amy Sara Carroll on "Topping from the Bottom"

What do this this piece hold for you?

"Topping from the Bottom: A Conversation with Kegels for Hegel and Patricia Montoya" en/treats love, lust, Latina/x/e sociality, the hyphenation of camp-rasquache. Ostensibly about the music video *Take Me to Yr Borderlands (Canción de amor a Gloria E. Anzaldúa)*, the piece more broadly addresses the queer, feminist and inter-American reading and remediation habits of Kegels for Hegel (Sarah Luna & Alexis Salas) and Patricia Montoya (and me!). Five years after this piece's publication, I imagine a more accurate subtitle for the piece might read, "Topping from the Bottom (Love Song to *and* with Kegels for Hegel and Patricia Montoya)." Better yet, "Topping from the Bottom" would be recognized as a collaboration, meaning authorship would be attributed to all four of us.

Originally published in February 2018 online at asterixjournal.com

Rodillas: A Kind of Reckoning

Daisy Hernández

I grew up believing that I belonged to a family of birds. When your family comes from Colombia, Cuba, Puerto Rico and Peru—the border is not a desert or a river but the entire sky. For years I thought of my family not as border crossers but as a flock of birds migrating north. The clouds kept secret that my mother and her sisters planned to overstay their tourist visas. The stars refused to snitch on my tía who hoped to find a doctor in New York to save her life. The sun only noticed that my tío fled further north.

When I read Gloria Anzaldúa's book *Borderlands/La Frontera,* however, I recognized her descriptions of the place where two nation states meet. I don't mean that I understood the metaphor. I mean I recognized an actual place. My family had never been a group of birds. We had a border. We had the aeropuerto.

The John F. Kennedy airport in the 1980s was full of knees. That is how the airport looked to me: a gathering of knobby knees and skinny knees and bulging rodillas. The knees filled the waiting area, a patch of land where the florescent lights flickered like a series of suns at dusk, and the men stood alone and stared at the door and the women sat in a row of plastic chairs with children who cried.

I grew up believing that I belonged to a family of birds. When your family comes from Colombia, Cuba, Puerto Rico and Peru—the border is not a desert or a river but the entire sky. For years I thought of my family not as border crossers but as a flock of birds migrating north. The clouds kept secret that my mother and her sisters planned to overstay their tourist visas. The stars refused to snitch on my tía who hoped to find a doctor in New York to save her life. The sun only noticed that my tío fled further north.

When I read Gloria Anzaldúa's book *Borderlands/La Frontera,* however, I recognized her descriptions of the place where two nation states meet. I don't mean that I understood the metaphor. I mean I recognized an actual place. My family had never been a group of birds. We had a border. We had the aeropuerto.

The John F. Kennedy airport in the 1980s was full of knees. That is how the airport looked to me: a gathering of knobby knees and skinny knees and bulging rodillas. The knees filled the waiting area, a patch of land where the florescent lights flickered like a series of suns at dusk, and the men stood alone and stared at the door and the women sat in a row of plastic chairs with children who cried.

Some of the knees tried to turn the waiting area into a party room. They brought bouquets of roses and white carnations, the tissue paper singing in their hands. They carried balloons in bright colors, and one time, a balloon escaped and bumped into the walls. Someone chased after it to no avail. We lost the balloon. Even though my mother had not brought the balloon, it felt like ours. The border did this to us. It turned strangers into first person plural. For a few hours, we belonged to the same country, the place of waiting for sisters, tías, husbands and cousins.

This is not to say that we agreed about the border. Some families came with balloons; my mother insisted on the dangers of el Kennedy. She had a round, pale face and a head of dark auburn hair. Her fingernails were polished, the color of pink salmon, and she sat in the plastic chair at JFK and clasped her hands and prayed, Ojalá, la dejen pasar. Ojalá, the doors will finally open. Ojalá, we won't have to wait much longer.

Sometimes we didn't wait for family but crossed the border ourselves. The year I was seven, we arrived at JFK from a three-week trip, and my mother sighed. She had to open the suitcases. Here, where Colombia met Nueva York, Mami had to peel back the foil on a container of arequipe so a white man with large hands could sniff the caramel. A flurry of English words erupted. He needed someone to speak Spanish. Here, the memory blurs. They found someone with enough words in Spanish to question my mother.

The man with the large hands returned the container, poked his fingers into our other bags. I was a child and I did not understand that flights from Colombia came with more than cafe and cheese. I didn't know how Colombia and all of Latin America rested in the hands of a few families there and the dictates of Washington. What I did know was that at the border white men with large hands could take what they wanted. Perhaps, it was an accurate observation of everything else.

Most of all, I remember the dog. A German shepherd, he glanced at me with empty black eyes, then poked his snout at the suitcases and at my sneakers. The leather leash slackened. I held my breath. I knew I was not allowed to touch the dog though I wanted to and was terrified to do so.

Daisy Hernández on "Rodillas"

How did this piece come about?

I wrote this short essay for a conference panel on Latinas writing about place. For a long time, I had wanted to write about the significance of airports for immigrant families, and I took this as the opportunity. My memories of waiting at JFK for tias shaped my sense of identity, and our arrivals and departures from that airport deeply influenced how I see borders today. When I started writing about the airport and waiting at those international doors, I almost immediately decided to focus on las rodillas, the knees of the adults around me, to clearly evoke that sense of a child's perspective.

Originally published in January 2017 online at asterixjournal.com

MEDIOCRITY IS THE SPACE WAITING TO BE FILLED BY ECCENTRICITY

Lucia Hierro

however meagre,

stuttering

with loose stitching

mediocrity is the space
waiting to be filled by eccentricity.

acute at this local
level—the perfect pointillism evoking
a remembered world in which detail itself seems precariously balanced between report and hallucination.

Intelligently, if not always profoundly

Lucia Hierro on "MEDIOCRITY IS THE SPACE WAITING TO BE FILLED BY ECCENTRICITY"

Share your reflections on this piece.

It has been 10 years since I looked at this work. Another artist was gaining recognition from a similar looking body of work of a more pressing matter. Instead of competing with it (though it had been the result of lots of hard work, personal and otherwise) I dropped the series all together.

Looking back at it I can see how I was readying myself to move forward with my larger than life concepts. There was still some fear and trepidation on how I would move forward. This work was a way to work through the many questions I have about how we see or overlook.

The New Yorker series itself was a meditative practice. I would force myself to read through the entire magazine. I'd go back to the articles I felt lent themselves to be deconstructed and reconstructed through a process of annotating, highlighting and redacting.

I think by now it's common knowledge that *The New Yorker* was made with a very particular reader in mind. I found myself in a really interesting position as a "DominicanYork" as well as an academic to play with the magazines presumption.

As someone who laments how little people read nowadays… to be honest… I romanticize the type of person who regularly sits and reads the whole magazine… despite its often exclusionary material and language.

I could not have imagined where these concepts of class and commentary on cultural consumption was going to take me but the sturdy bones were there.

Originally published in our Fall 2020 issue, *The Ferrante Project*

The Patient Records
Ferrante Project

1.

It begins in the middle like this: the sun sets quietly in a Brooklyn sky. From the top of a hill we can see the Statue of Liberty signaling an idealism long squashed out from our hearts. Even so, trust does not leave the body completely, and I, floating between intent and the unwritten book, am about to hold my hand out to a young man for a prescription drug no doctor will prescribe for me, even though I need it. Instead, they prescribe me medicines I don't want and that don't work.

2.

It's 2017 and I make my way to a section of the borough I have not been to before—somewhere bordering Williamsburg and Bushwick. A nervous kid about eighteen years old meets me in a regular New York deli across from some housing projects. Our agreement is thirty 20 mg pills of Adderall in exchange for $180. I am nervous too. *I need the money first,* he says, holding a prescription bottle tight in his hand. *You don't get the money first,* I say, *I need to see the pills to make sure they are real.* He fidgets. It feels like a setup, so I leave empty-handed. I return to the comfort of my car and experience a familiar sensation, like I can feel the blood in my veins, adrenaline racing, the life of living. Anything can happen. The kid appears at my car window. *Get in the car,* I tell him, so I can make sure you're not trying to rip me off. He says he can't get into a stranger's car. He is my height, regular male build for his age, but he probably thinks that I am the police and I am thinking that he is the police. *This isn't going to work*, I say, and speed off.

3.

That feeling that anything can happen at any time is a condition inscribed into my body by the many things that happened to me as kid. Nothing was within my control then and because of this fact I began to understand the randomness of things occurring. A squirrel, for example, can fall from a thin branch the instant you walk under it right onto your face. There's simply no way to plan for things or avoid other things. This is a revolting way of experiencing the world, but I'm also attracted to it. It's a survival strategy. So when the drug dealer sends me a text that says, *That wasn't me. I sent my brother, and my brother can't do anything right*, I rush back in to meet a new guy and a revised scam. The presence of the drug dealer and my acting beyond the boundaries of reason surely signal, to the reader, an addiction; I understand this. I don't know how to make a compelling case for some other relationship to the drugs I'm trying and failing to obtain.

4.

A certain difficulty lies in the difference between what we want and what we need. Conventional wisdom would have it that in order to differentiate between desire and requirement one must first be able access the past using memory. You have to figure out when memory is about a real happening, a pure feeling, or comes from made-up thoughts. For Freud, memory determines much of who we are (the beingness of being). When one has access to recalled memory, it presents, first, I think, in images and then the brain kicks in to do its interpretation work. We like to think about our memories. We like to ask questions about what occurred, about what we don't remember or what was outside of the frame entirely. Want can only come from the mind, if you buy into this theory, and what we know about ourselves and believe ourselves to remember, while need is more precise, I think, but also more suspect. The body can have its own needs including, but not limited to, the nutrients that one must have for survival. But, when another person says, *I need you*, we think they are really referring to desire.

5.

I have a memory, akin to one you have, maybe, from a photograph in my mother's photo album. I'm about three years old, dressed for church—it might be Easter—in a light blue dress and cape, and holding an open yellow umbrella above my head. It appears to me that I look forlorn and I remember keenly a forlorn feeling, trapped in the outfit and white tights and black patent-leather Mary Janes. My mother loved Mary Janes in her own youth and nostalgically purchased them for me, attempting, it seems, to hold on to time. She loves old-fashioned candy like Squirrel Nut Zippers and records on vinyl and Charlie Pride, born one year after her, and the Grand Ole Opry on the radio. I do not remember wearing the dress, but I do remember the house I'm standing in front of in the photo. It was in a part of town that my parents wanted to get away from, and did eventually, touching down in a part of town more integrated, which meant better.

6.

I no longer remember being inside of the child body dressed in soft blue, but I can still feel its precarious existence, and its knowing, even so, a possible power that might be accessed. One day, when I was older, four or five, I was playing outside on the old metal railing in front of the house's side door. When I fell from the railing, I did so in a way where I landed on my child vagina, my legs splayed on either side of the bar. I had done this to myself but now it would have to be investigated, which meant exposure of a part of my body I hadn't yet thought about in any significant way. In moments like these, one becomes the body's flesh, skeletal scaffold, and blood. I imagine this child-body laid out on a silver examining table, under a stark gaze, yet somehow invisible. My mother wanted to check to see if I was bleeding given that the fall had caused me to wail hysterically, inconsolably. I don't remember if I was taken to the doctor or what happened after. I remember nothing else except a shadow feeling of being in the kind of pain that happens to bones.

7.

Time is not linear; instead it's like a strong breath tunneling up through experience and spreading out, inhabiting a body. A body can be infinite as much as it's a mechanism for processing food. When my mother tells me a story, it's as if time has stood still for her. No partition between the past and the future. No influence of one upon the other. She glances around her present surroundings, a vacant look in her eyes, and tells me about the time her uncle pulled a gun on some white men asking for directions. *They weren't asking for directions,* she says with a tilt of the head. It was night. A gas station somewhere way out in swamplands. I can picture those white men and the goofy frivolity of their violence and my mother's uncle and whoever else was in the car like apparitions in the room. One person's good-old-boy fun is another person's dismemberment, is their dogged haunting. I, too, am trying to concentrate on something outside of time.

8.

I tell you all of this—the fall from the railing, the nonmemory of wearing the blue dress, the man with his hand shaking, likely, around a rifle pointed at some white guys' heads—as a way of blurring the distinction between desire and need and highlighting the possibility for nonlinear time. Also, I want you to know me better. Those memories and not-memories are also ways for me to three-dimensionalize the depths of my person as a character in this narrative. But here's some advice: don't try to talk to a medical professional about nonlinear time. The professions are there to tell you what you need and to disparage what you know to be true. I am very uncertain about the function of memories of the past and how they work if time is not a thing that we are simply marching through, or that's marching through us. It can be challenging to develop your own idea of things when regulated by professionals' bright laboratories. Those professionals with their badges of knowledge will look directly at the burning sore on your asshole and tell you that it cannot be from the medication they prescribed you. It's a fungus, they tell you, cause unknown, produced by the body of its own accord. The badge-wearers tell you to take another medicine to cure the fungus, but they don't tell you that the other medicine can make you sterile. Or, you enter the emergency medical center with a sore throat, and the doctors—two of them—say it's probably gonorrhea and that you should probably get antibiotic injections right now before the test results come back. Your mouth falls open. You are 99 percent sure that you do not have gonorrhea of the throat but for a minute you actually consider the injections.

9.

All the ways your body is a site for investigation, someone else's false documentary. Many years ago, when I was a graduate student, I accepted my psychiatrist's invitation to participate in an ADHD study. The psychiatrist and I had the relationship that most patients have with their mental health doctors. I was under his care. In his care I could help him understand things about medicines for the mind. Or, at the very least, the way these medicines worked or did not work on me. It seemed like he was trying to find the perfect balance of medications to help me. He did this by changing my medicines and dosages periodically in a similar way that I might, not being a doctor. When I entered the ADHD study, I was hungover most of the time. No one asked me if I was hungover, and I wonder now if this influenced the result of the study. The psychologist who administered the tests—twenty hours of them—was very kind but had distractingly small hands and feet, like a child's. Rather conclusively, the psychologist with the tiny extremities determined that I did not have ADHD. She became my therapist after that, and I would sit in her office once once a week, telling her some things but not others, mostly looking at the child-sized rain boots on the corner mat. I didn't tell her about the vaginal wound. I thought she might read too much into it. Or the wrong things. She liked to view most things through the lens of conflict. She would say, If there's not a conflict there's not a problem. My primary problems were a deep sadness, anxiety, and also that I was having a lot of anonymous sexual encounters. I call them "encounters" because they weren't sex exactly. And the people didn't feel like people. It was mostly jerking off and inappropriate touching, sometimes with force: all sex games with pre-articulated rules. We met in secret, barely trafficked places. The encounters struck me as dangerous and the danger rose in my blood, propelling me toward the faceless, nameless bodies. The conflict was that I was doing something potentially harmful but I was unsure whether I wanted to be harmed.

10.

The anonymous sexual encounters were situated somewhere between need and want. They were also a way toward a reckoning, peeling back the skin to see what's underneath, what you're really made of. No one told me to do it. The actions just occurred to my body. I began to avoid all the other activities in my life, which became tatters around the edges, whispering my name. The encounters are how I know what I know about time, how it can shrink down inside itself and become like a black hole in outer space even as a day, for instance, turns from light to dark. I learned another thing, more practical, about how the creatures you meet in the dark are not all monsters. Or maybe the converse was my true education—that monsters often inhabit the light, look just like rest of us, have regular jobs. Their monstrous acts appear small and relatively harmless.

11.

Once a month I went to the psychiatrist, the one with the prescriptions. He didn't ask me about conflict or how I spent my days. He asked me how I was feeling. I couldn't focus on anything. The depressed state was alleviated but persisted. I thought I wanted to live. The stars of this imaginary documentary, the one about my body but not me, are two doctors whose offices are located in different buildings. They peer into the same test-tube body yet never speak to each other, secure in their individual conclusions. If I had known that a body can become a kind of object as it seeks relief, I would have told them both what they needed to know so that they could write a joint paper. It would recommend listening outside of what they think they know about the mind and memory and the uncertain balance of anyone's psyche. I knew, for example, that the conclusion from the ADHD tests was incorrect. I didn't know how to tell them that the fire that occupied me when my body was in potential danger was evidence to this fact. In other words, when my heart raced, when adrenaline pulsed through my veins, focus and calm kicked in, a feeling of equilibrium. I do not mean this to be evidence, but discovery. An internal landscape, partially mapped.

12.

My mother provides evidence in the false documentary. Standing outside of time, she is young and thin again, on a beach boardwalk with her sister, wearing a one-piece bathing suit and sunhat, smiling. What she does not know in this moment is that she will marry a man who will move her thousands of miles away from her family and that this man will not love her, nor she him. She tells the doctors, *I have a girl child in your future. The girl child is an intellectual.* She reads and reads. My mother does not know about the fire like a hot poker pressing inside my belly. The knowledge evades her in any configuration of time. I am beyond her world partitioned by the contours of a small body in view and the believed wholesomeness of a girl's existence: this, whatever I am.

13.

I know better now than to ask any doctor for what I need, lest it be confused with want. There is nothing left for memory in service of medicine. If you give them your memories, they'll likely see the prefigured drawings carved into their textbooks. What is held in the secret, mysterious spaces of our bodies? Throughout my entire childhood, I got nosebleeds of the epic sort. They came on suddenly, blood pouring out of my nose like a warning, until a washcloth filled with ice placed on the bridge of my nose slowed the bleeding and big clots formed that I'd snort out. There are some researchers who write about what the body holds, and what that holding does to the body and the mind. They tell us that the body holds trauma and doesn't even know it because that holding produces an extreme disconnect from the body. And, even so, the body has to deal with that stress situation of trauma, and we can't know what that will be like inside each person. Still, not everything is known.

14.

The ways toward transformation are mysterious. That a partial healing of the psyche occurred in whatever tangential way it happened, outside of medical prescriptions and the doctors' claims about care, surprised me. It was intuition that drove me to allow strangers the sexual use of my body, even though I sometimes called that intuition "compulsion." And it was this compulsion that enabled a purging. Something had been stuck inside my body, and I needed to work it out. The need for danger may have been a desire for death. The overindulgence in the courting of death moved through me because it had nowhere else to go. Free from it, I could focus on my actual sexual desires, not the driving obligations that felt like service instruments, but the ones that lived deep inside my being. The instruments allowed me to eject a good deal of vaginal hurt. Vaginal hurt, in this case, is a vast landscape of pain that includes what has been inflicted on the gendered body (female) and the vulnerable availability of the child body. I was still in therapy at the time and visiting the psychiatrist for pills. Once I could feel myself on the other side of my obscene and secret process, I fired them both and stopped taking all the medicines.

15.

Years go by. All around me, change. I watch the boy next door grow into a young man. I accomplish some things. Post-medication, I have to relearn how to feel the range of what's to be felt. Anxiety and depression occasionally still send me into days of waste. The first time I take an ADHD drug it's recreationally. A friend gives me Adderall to take in any way I want. I don't yet know their power, and I take one at a conference in Boston during a blizzard. Imagine the knee-deep snow and more falling heavy like stones, blinding wind, the conference-goers stumbling around and falling in the middle of streets, everyone underdressed in a weird state of disbelief. But for me, it's the first time in years when I haven't had to binge on alcohol in order to negotiate an intense social situation. Suddenly, the excitement of it all does not overwhelm. I feel okay. Like, I feel fine in an even way. I'm in place, which is to say, the snow is beautiful.

16.

I found my way onto the dark web after Dr. R, a psychiatrist who only does video conferencing, convinced me that I should try Cymbalta. This was after I had clearly communicated to her that I did not want to take long-term antidepressants because it had taken me years to wean myself off them when I fired my doctors back in graduate school. I told her this before the video meeting and again at the meeting itself, which was before she charged my credit card $400, if you're still interested in conventional notions of time. Stupidly, I had also told her that my preferred medicine was for ADHD, that I found it calming. I had expressed my needs. I had drawn a line in the sand. This is what we've been told to do as women, to be empowered agents of our own destinies, yes?

17.

Ignoring this request, she did a good talking up of Cymbalta's possibilities. She seemed like she'd long been practicing the contortion of the face to appear empathetic. Same goes for her intonation. I was having a hard time seeing things as they were, and her performance created a tiny bubble of hope in the center of my throat. The hope bubble popped almost immediately because one introductory dose of Cymbalta turned me into a zombie. My arms and legs buzzed, but at the same time I couldn't feel them. A pall was pulled down over the space between me and everything outside my body. I could scream, *There's someone alive in here!*, but no one would hear me. Dr. R, via a texting mechanism associated with the video-conferencing mechanism, said that I could be "a little tired" for up to two weeks but then I'd feel better. This was a lie. People on message boards talked about debilitating fatigue lasting months. They were stuck in the space between living and dying, with only those like them—or those afraid of becoming them—to listen to their claims of discomfort. I had a book to finish. Dr. R knew this, but she didn't seemed to understand that there's a symbiotic relationship between the creative mind at work and the transformation of psychic pain. The rest of the pills are tucked in the recesses of my medicine cabinet, if you want them. I told Dr. R that I had to find a psychiatrist with more imagination—one who did not insist, for instance, that there was no evidence that microdosing LSD or hallucinogenic mushrooms can have an effect on existential ailments that dig out the psyche. There is something beyond Freud and Lacan and Jung, my mother, the ego, the pathology of desire, and anchor events. I wanted to believe Dr. R, but she wanted to schedule another $400 meeting.

18.

One Virtual Private Network (VPN), one Bitcoin account, and one TOR search engine later, and I'm on the dark web where, admittedly, some of the most horrible beings on God's green earth lurk and organize and build connections toward some unimaginable catastrophe. But the mechanism itself is not monstrous, however much it allows for the worst of humanity to indulge in brutality. The dark expansive wildernesses of Mississippi are not responsible for the bloodshed, lynchings, and cutting of genitalia. It's a mutated kind of person who makes the sacred land a wet burial ground for murdered lambs. And what to do when you must enter the wild forests at night anyway? They provide your cloak, too, as scary and risky as it all is.

19.

In your future, a small package will arrive stuffed into the mailbox.

No return address. The package contains four small capsules hidden in the lining of a disposable garment. They are individually packaged by the manufacturer. No matter the signs that seem to point toward the drug's legitimacy, you have a panic attack immediately after your test run when you open one of the capsules and pour some of the contents into your mouth. You begin sweating and you feel like you're going to pass out. It's poison, a voice from nowhere says. Oh my God, I'm dying, another voice in your head screams. The voices quiet when death doesn't come stabbing. About forty-five minutes later, you're sitting on your patio writing this very essay and feeling quite at ease.

20.

A friend once told me that her mother is the quintessentially Indian mother, meaning that her mother's goal is to anticipate and fulfill her children's needs before they even know they have them. That seems impossible, I told my friend. What if she anticipates incorrectly? To me it sounded like a fictional creation of the child's reality, a planting of foreign seeds into a consciousness, a means toward control. I told my friend this, too, insensitive to any cultural notions beyond my experience. I went even further: It seems very colonialist, I said. I think of the girl in the photo at Easter. All the props that construct that image. A camera's lens often shirks its responsibility of transparency. In this case, however, the image profoundly reveals the erasure of the girl. Someone had asked that I place one hand on my hip, because there the hand is on the hip; the other hand holds the yellow umbrella, though it is not raining. But I have never willingly placed my hand on my hip for a photo.

21.

Rebellion happens in my eyes, which refuse to look up at the camera; my head is cast slightly downward, as if to say simply, *No*. If I am creating my own story, and I guess I am, the sunken forests, darknets, and shaded eyes are not where I gather my strength for resistance. It is here, in the light, with all of you, on the airy side of the blinded window alongside the micromonsters and everything else.

22.

In the dcumentary I make of myself, I am lying on a beach where time is slowed and stretched out, making the body soft like blue light. My mother tells me for the hundredth time that she told her primary care physician for the hundredth time that the injections they gave her have made her crippled. She's stuck inside this conversation that begins, I know what caused my pain, and ends with the doctor saying, There is no reason for your pain. I am reminded of Joan Didion's reporting in *The White Album* about Huey Newton being shot in the stomach, and the trial of Newton that follows. In the transcript of the trial, a nurse tells of his refusal to prove his insurance coverage and sign documents as he is bleeding from the gunshot wound. The nurse claims that even though he has been shot in that sensitive organ, he's not in any "acute distress." The presence of the human body and its language do not provide good evidence, apparently, about the experience of the person, depending on who that person is.

23.

My mother and I time-travel, in my documentary, to a far-flung coast on the Mediterranean Sea to talk to each other. In this way, we escape time and its trappings. We escape the world that claims to know us better than we know ourselves. I tell her that once I tried to buy ADHD drugs from a fake drug dealer in Bed Stuy who cheated me and gave me allergy meds instead.Nobody was listening to me,I tell her,so I had to listen to the sound of my own heart. What do I want from her, my mother, outside of time and the labor of her sagging living room where, in the other world, she always is? We doze a little in our chaise lounges, the ocean rhythms like the beat of existence. When we wake, she says, *There are so many ways that they don't see us, just as I've never seen you.*

Originally published in our Fall 2018 issue, *Edges*

March

Shayla Lawz

L tells me that her grandmother has died. I keep hold of the water. I see my grandmother in the mirror. I keep hold of the water. The plant dies. I keep hold of the water. I accept it.   I keep hold of the water. I want to be home. I keep hold of the water. I want to be here. I keep hold of the water. I want here to be home. I keep hold of the water. I want to be home. I keep hold of the water.

Originally published in our Spring 2014 issue,
Ra(i)ces: Black Feminist Encounters

"I will carry a knife and always it in my mouth"

LaTasha N. Nevada Diggs

"I will carry a knife and always it in my mouth." – Fátima Portorreal

here looking for bones. huesos. unborn generations within fossil coral
ancient mud
flanked by wood. engineered madera. stone. piedra

nurse & herald. on luscious lands both victim & captor

my ancestor frightens me
because she is unafraid to show her face
where I lay

Elmina Castle is across the waters. messengers cemented inside deep
prefitted gates. prepped for rape & market. Elmina is a Ghanian
patchwork skirt.

amarillo for Dutch. bricks archival. rojo for Portuguese.
dents are muscle & roof tiles. this scent a troubled question.
authenticity. re/installment. renovation. restored terrences

I am afraid here because polished replaced rock conceals something.

at *Ingenio Boca de Nigua,* the lack of putrid molasses makes ghosts of
Mastiffs louder. they are in chase of Wolof & Canary skeletons rising

still shackled to their Catholic priests. I hear every bite wail clang fist

here lost in sediments my ancestor is of these *worthless* Caribs
those Congolese,
them Guineans,
that Angolan

despite her womanhood crowned with bayahibe,
battered feet, wide & flat carry denial's weight.

she makes the blood & chains obvious.

this damaged fistula.
that hemorrhage.
this embolism.
these severed heads. infections gone septic

upon hearing the palmchat mixed sand & brick
here she stands uncrushed by the sugar's capicé
a metaphor never swinging at the Door of Mercy

who says "sin hombre, she is useless because she converses with spirits"?
   this border's fragility is not as fierce

my ancestor is assembling the bones of Ana Maria.
this warrior is rattling the grave of Mama Tingo.
my mother is pulling from rubble

Myriam Merlet, Magalie Marcelin
Anne Marie Coriolan, Nicole Grégoire, Gina Dorcena, Mirland
Dorvilus, Bernardine Bourdeau

all of her names are remedy.
names heavy on tits exhumed from nightmares
y sin hombre, she is preparing the body of Sonia Pierre
for a proper burial
while Cardinals aspire to burn the names of those
whose spit polish the kitchen tiles & secular marble
sin hombre, she is Atabey, cradling the stillborn children of children
named Lucia

the centurion witches of Batey fear her. politicians lose sleep.

with her fishing net, sin hombre, she drags the sea in search of more
ancestors
who one by one, speak to her in tongues, in dreams, in flight.

my ancestor frightens me
because she is unafraid to show her face
where I lay.

I didn't know then that each security dog is worth thousands of dollars. That they are trained, like soldiers, in a school in Texas, run by the Defense Department.

What I did know was that we had to scale the wall: the dog, the white man, the entire airport. With Gloria's book, I learned that some places cannot be crossed. Some places become a part of who you are, become like your neck or your knees: a kind of reckoning.

Originally published in May 2020 online at asterixjournal.com

---

NON-ESSENTIAL KNOWLEDGE: LATINX STUDIES IN TIMES OF COVID-19

Lorgia Garcia Pena

Writing at the turn of the twentieth century, Arthur Schomburg, the black Puerto Rican scholar and bibliophile, advocated for the creation of departments of Black History, and for the formation of Black historians as a way to contrast the lies, the silences and the outright violence produced about black and brown people in the university. I have written on multiple occasions about the significance of Schomburg's proposal to re-introduce that which "slavery took away:" the possibility of humanity and belonging as a prelude to Ethnic Studies — Black, Latinx, Indigenous, Asian, Islamic — as an early articulation for an anti-colonial, anti-white supremacist space of knowledge production and learning.

Schomburg was a black Puerto Rican man, an idealist and an entrepreneur who very much believed in the possibility of freedom and equality for all people. When he migrated to New York City at the end of the nineteenth century, he did so because he wanted to join the revolutionary efforts to free Puerto Rico from Spanish colonial exploitation.

In New York, however, he soon found himself in the "belly of the beast", to borrow José Martí's famous phrase. U.S. colonialism swallowed up Puerto Rico and spat him out a non-citizen migrant, a different kind of black man. It was hard enough to be a black man in the world, but to be a black migrant? That was an insurmountable burden. Schomburg, despite his incredible success, always lived in between two forms of unbelonging: black and migrant. Although Schomburg did not define himself as an Afro-Latino or Latinx, partly because those were not terms available to him at the turn of the twentieth century, his experience with race, migration and unbelonging are relevant to many of us who identify as Black or brown Latinx today. Whether born in the U.S. or elsewhere, our racialized bodies, our Hispanic last names, our accents, and our immigrant experiences continue to exclude many of us from Americanness: We are Latinx, Latina/os, and in this country, in this political climate, that is a mark of unbelonging and exclusion.

Reading Schomburg's work, however, one cannot help but feel a flash of optimism and hope. This man was ahead of his times: He articulated black diaspora before the term existed. He connected the dots of U.S. colonialism in the Pacific and the Caribbean, marking those connections as producing second-class citizenship as early as 1901. And, he saw that the only way to a future of "racial integrity" was through transnational forms of anti-colonial solidarity grounded on knowledge, on history, on the possibility of another way of learning. Schomburg wrote:

The white scholar's mind and heart are fired because in the temple of learning they are told how on March 5, 1770 the Americans were able to beat the English; but to find Crispus Attucks it is necessary to go deep into special books…Where is our historian to give us our side of view? We need in the coming dawn the man who will give us **the background of our future**; it matters not whether he comes from the cloisters of the university or from the rank and file of the fields.

Schomburg dedicated his life to building the largest archive of black histories and left it there for us to build upon it, to write books with and about, to teach from, to fuel the black scholar's mind. His work, his life, his archive were built on the hope that we would grab the torch and keep on moving. Some of us have tried.

Over the past decade of teaching Latinx Studies at various institutions— Dartmouth College, the University of Georgia, Harvard University, Freedom University— I have seen what Schomburg meant by "kindling the torch of knowledge and racial integrity." Semester after semester, as my courses filled with first-generation, mostly Latinx students of different racial, national and economic backgrounds, coming from both the "cloisters of the university and the rank of the fields" I marveled at their empowerment after reading, thinking and producing work through the frameworks of anti-colonial Latinx and Ethnic Studies. The dozens of letters and emails from students over these years with words like: "This class saved me" or "reading Josefina Baez changed my life" have been tangible reminders of the importance of doing anti-colonial Latinx and ethnic studies work, not only in terms of building the "background of the future" and "kindling the torches" of knowledge as Schomburg hoped we would, but also in creating spaces for survival and community within the colonial, violent structures of higher education which continues to produce Latinx lives, Latinx knowledge, Latinx faculty and Latinx students as non-essential, as extras in the perfectly orchestrated machinery of the corporate university system.

The Covid-19 crisis has brought to light a multiplicity of crises—the fragility of capitalism, the precariousness of our medical system, the inadequacy of our public health system, the insufficiency of social services unable to adequately provide relief from food stamps to unemployment benefits. Meaning, it has also brought to light—for those who had the privilege of not knowing—the enormous inequality that exists in this world between those who have a lot and those who do not. Ironically, the latter now includes part of a new category of human beings we are calling "essential": workers who must continue to risk their lives and die in order to provide the services the rest of us need to survive. It is no surprise to anyone that these workers are Latinx, that they are migrants, that they are Black, that they are poor. They are also my students' parents, my students' brothers, my students' sisters. They are my students.

The university has not been immune to the Covid-19 pandemic. As a corporation, as part of the capitalist machinery, the university has seen many loses all too quickly. Hires have been frozen, workers laid off, aid cut; we are all bracing ourselves for the worse that is yet to come. Even as they face financial stress, universities continue to assure students that the integrity of their education will be preserved, that knowledge-making and learning will continue.

At Harvard, where I created and direct the Latinx Secondary, a graduate student certificate that currently serves 24 students from across the university, I see the impact up close. The years of precarity and neglect of Latinx Studies, paired with tenure denials, inability to retain Latinx faculty and the freeze on hire has left my students without a structured Latinx studies program beginning next fall, despite the university's commitment to "excellence in learning and teaching." Likewise, across the United States, searches in Ethnic Studies and Latinx Studies have been cancelled or put on hold. No one protests. We say nothing. We are amidst a crisis and there is nothing that we can do. Students must adapt, study something else, find a way to learn on their own. Teach themselves their own histories. It is a crisis. It is a pandemic. People are dying and Latinx Studies is non-essential.

Except it is.

Before the pandemic there was another crisis

Anti-colonial ethnic studies— Black, Latinx, Indigenous, Asian, Islamic Studies— is charged with the immeasurable task of filling the gaps left by all the other fields of knowledge, with creating a learning environment that contrasts the supremacy of whiteness, inequality, racism, and exclusion that dominates our canons, libraries, and archives. Through the lens and the framework of ethnic studies, future doctors, lawyers, teachers, public servants and business people learn a more ethical, more just way to live, to create, to serve one another. What could possibly be more essential to our humanity as the very people represented in the fields of ethnic studies are dying, as their bodies are sent to the front lines to be sacrificed? What could possibly be more essential to our universities than to provide the opportunity for learning about this crisis from within, from the very experiences of those who are most affected by it, from the knowledge that comes from the "file of the fields"?

Before Covid-19, before March 2020, college students across the United States mobilized in support of ethnic studies, in demand of better conditions for graduate students and in protests against racism, misogyny and inequality across campuses. At Harvard, students demanded for ethnic studies programs and courses. They also demanded clarity around tenure denials of professors of color, including my own tenure denial. Cross-country, at Stanford, students asked "Who is teaching us?" in an effort to raise awareness about the lack of faculty diversity on campus. At Yale, students were demanding departmentalization of ethnic studies, faculty resources, and clarity around tenure denial of Latinx studies faculty. The list could go on and on, beyond the Ivy League. As we celebrated the fiftieth anniversary of the creation of the first ethnic studies Program in San Francisco State, other schools were still fighting to retain the single faculty member devoted to ethnic studies scholarship, to hire a second person, to create at least a minor in the field. All the asks fell on the deaf ears of the institutions because like our people, our field is deemed non-essential.

As I experienced in my own skin the disavowal of Latinx Studies (and by extension ethnic studies) in the very institution where I'd worked to build it for seven years, I went back to Schomburg, to his call for "kindling the torches of knowledge", for building departments and programs, for teaching against the white supremacy of the university even if from within the belly of the beast. I continue to wonder, where did we go wrong? How are we, one hundred years later, STILL having this fight? Why do we STILL need to convince our institutions that this knowledge is indeed essential, that our students do matter, that our work has value in this world?

Dylan Rodriguez said it best: "Ethnic Studies represents some of the most transformative, epistemologically and theoretically challenging, critically and publicly engaged work to emerge from the academy in the last half century. In producing such field—and academy—altering work, Ethnic Studies represents the elite research university's (e.g. Harvard et. al.'s) antithesis." How can the university promote, reward and support a field whose very purpose is to dismantle the structures on which the very institution is grounded? Like Schomburg at the turn of the twentieth century, Latinx Studies and Ethnic Studies live within the belly of the beast. As scholars in these fields, we produce knowledge, create spaces, and teach in contra*diction* to our institutions, to the colonial, oppressive structures of the white-supremacist university. As such, our work, our people, our students, are chewed up and spat out if we are not subtle enough, if we upset the belly, if our work becomes too essential. So where do we go from here? How do we continue amidst this violence?

Let us go back to Schomburg. One of his most incredible propositions was that of "a nation without a nation," a concept we now understand as diaspora. For Schomburg, however, the idea of having this transnational solidarity nation, did not mean he gave up his place within the U.S. American nation. He strived to create an alternative place of belonging as he continued to push within the belly, making space for himself amidst the discomfort. We need to do the same. If I have learned anything over the past decade, and particularly, over this past year, it is to not trust institutions, to not believe in the systems that were not ever meant to sustain me. It is an insurmountable task to work, to care, to teach and to produce knowledge while living and working through this violence. And yet we do, and we must. But we must also find other ways, we must also create our own "nations without nations," our own institutions without institutions, our collectives of joy and learning where our work and our lives are always properly recognized as essential.

Originally published in our Fall 2016 issue, *What We Love*

list of things to say instead of "I'm fine"

Marlin M. Jenkins

my blood moves like tectonic plates: so slow
one might not notice, but notice first, please,
before the earthquake.

*

i have always been afraid of waves, how they say:
i know *what it's like*
to crumble *over myself and*
hear my crashing simply
called *beautiful*

*

the syncopation of my heart's   swung notes
is more than   metronome.
but
not quite a full   song, either.

*

i woke up this morning

as a houseplant not watered
in weeks. when i tried
to move, wilted pieces
of brown flesh crumbled
onto the carpet, waited
there for the vacuum.

*

i am tired   of how this skin
makes lonely, how afraid i am
that i'll say i'm   black
and scared   and no one
will listen—that i will say
i am proud   and be
perceived therefore as threat.

*

today is that ice cube song,
but because a good day means
so much forgetting.

*

something in this city
is always on fire. before
the neighbor's car it was
the house around the corner.
before that, the trash can
on the curb the night
before garbage day.

*

remember playing *the floor is lava*?
like that, except the lava is also
the walls and ceiling and furniture.

maybe moses' feet were burned
when he removed
his sandals at the feet of the bush.
what saint has not lived
constant pain?

*

hansel and gretel left
bread crumbs when they should have
left a trail of blood,
held their faces   down and
admitted they were lost.

*

i no longer have to meet yearly
with the cardiologist. i will not miss
the tug of ekg stickers pulling off
body hair, but i miss the jelly on chest,
the dull pressure of the instrument
pressing skin around ribs and sternum,
to see my center on a screen—
yes, there are parts in here
that are pumping,
working, despite.

Marlin M. Jenkins on "list of things to say instead of 'I'm fine'"

What shaped the piece, and how do you feel now?

This poem came from a moment of being consistently "not fine" and trying to be more honest about it--both with others and with myself. But the sources of the feeling were complex and many, so no one response felt right, and I wanted to play with the idea of multiple versions of a response all being true at the same time, even if they ranged in style and content. So much has changed since I wrote this poem, but it feels like a moment that unlocked something in my writing with how I try to approach authenticity--and I'm so glad the poem has found readers over time who have felt seen by it.

Originally published in our Fall 2017 issue, *Dirty Laundry*

Tlaquaches

Joe Jimenez

i.

I don't recall the first time I saw a tlaquache, an opossum, though I do remember the first memory I carry of one. Tucked inside me, an assemblage of ideas behind my heart, maybe, or just under it, left in that dry dirt, in the weeds of things I do not like to think about but, even with effort, cannot forget. An alley, maybe a monte, an abandoned lot, a room, maybe a shed or a pouch, a field of dark mud, some realm inside us that shoulders our shadows—I think each of us carries such a place.

In the summer, after wanting very badly to, I read the opening to Édouard Louis's The End of Eddy, and I remembered, then, horribly, while laying in my bed, while cuddling my small hairless dog who died at the end of that summer, I remembered my mother's boyfriend, and I remembered that small opossum on the fence one night when I was very young, and I remembered the baseball bat, a man's bulging brown arm, the look of bonecrush and gutcry, the grown man's full-muscled swings.

In the opening of Louis's novel, we are told about the boy's father and we are told about their poverty and their hardships and his queerness growing up in a small French town, and I remember all of this, having identified very much with its shadows, even if my own life came about half a world away. We are told that the boy himself is soft in the ways that boys like us can be soft, and also, we are told the boy's father is cruel, an attribute, a behavior, a routine proven so early in the novel by the father's resolution to his problem of the stray cat that stayed near the house having kittens. So early in that story, Louis tells us the father places the stray's kittens in a plastic bag and slams the bag, the bag with small kittens inside it, against the brick wall. Again, again, he does this. Again, again, he kills them. Until there were no more cries. A resolution, perhaps for the father, ridding himself of these kittens. Yet, resolution for someone often leads to irresolution for another—as it so often plays out, someone's light is ultimately someone else's great darkness.

I do not have to tell you my mom's boyfriend was a real asshole; I do not have to tell you all the shit things he did to my family. But I will tell you that all of the world is stark naked, it is, at some point, when no one or when everyone is watching .

Yes, that night, I saw men kill a tlaquache. Yes, they used a baseball bat. Yes, it was brutal. Those men laughed and they laughed, yes. I was twelve, thirteen, maybe. A strange place, that age, that place of a boy's life, with the children in the bedroom playing a game and the women around the table laughing and laughing, swallowing their beer, and the men being men in the trees under the streetlights, their long tongues, their sweat, like their stories, building lies of the real men they were and how each, via his tale, held membership in the clan.

Afterward, away from them, behind my mom's boyfriend's grey truck parked on the street, when no one was watching, I squatted down to my knees, and holding my fists over my eyes, I imagined what had happened to the small opossum's body, which lay, then, on the other side of the fence, in an alley, where they'd pitched its battered body when they were done with it. In my throat, my curled heart. In my heart, a heat I've encountered only a few other times in my life. Call it rage, call it clarity, call it brownness and queerness. And while I could hear them joking near the barbecue pit, I tried not to think of it, and I promised myself I would grow stronger than them all one day—with my heart in my mouth, I tried not to think of taking a baseball bat to each one of those shitty men.

ii.

I cannot say that I have always loved tlaquaches. They are not like hummingbirds or jaguars—there is no glamor to a tlaquache. Hummingbirds are magical, of course. The fury of their marvelous wings, their iridescent green coats, their red throats. Jaguars, also, with their magnificence, their predatory prowess, their status as warrior symbol, are easy to love or fear, maybe admire, perhaps all of these potencies at once. But tlaquaches are not like hummingbirds or jaguars. Tlaquaches are opossums. They live under our houses, in dilapidated sheds, in great montes, we find their bodies in or the by the sides of roads—they eat ticks, they carry their young on their backs, they lay in the hot sun in the middle of a street or road and die and are run over again and again, if no one picks them up. If they are picked up, frequently, their bodies are frequently trashed. There is no burial, no grief for tlaquaches.

iii.

Behind my heart, or just under it, left in that dry dirt, in the weeds of things I do not like to think about—I am not a good man, I fear. But even not-good men deserve love and want it.

If I say it, will I believe it? If I write it, will you believe me?

iv.

When my husband and I moved in together, he expressed horror over the fact that I knew a tlaquache lived under our house. It is an old house made of wood, with too many rooms, and two fireplaces, one of which is now buried in one of the walls. Since 2008, I'd lived in the house, having left for two years, but returning with my new husband, after my second lover took his life. The house was built in 1925. It is a large house, and true to the time period, it stands atop piers and beams. There is a crawl space, and to access the crawl space, there is a small wooden door on two grey hinges. The door is the size of a large shoebox, maybe one for keeping boots or Stetson hats. Plumbers and electricians have entered the crawl space to perform work underneath the house, and late at night, after walking dogs or upon parking in the driveway, I have seen cats and skunks and tlaquaches using this door. My husband also saw the opossum, one night, pushing its grey body beneath this door, out into the rest of the world. My husband gave it no second thought: he wanted it gone.

v.

The first man I ever loved was not an animal lover. But he loved me, perhaps more than any other human ever has, perhaps more than he loved even himself.

The second man? An animal lover who once, as a boy, rescued a raccoon he called Bandit, and in our time together, also rescued a young blind skunk one dusk, keeping her in one of the bathrooms in our house, and he fed her and cradled her until I convinced him that her best chance lay not with us but with an animal refuge an hour outside of San Antonio. He wept the whole drive home after we dropped her off.

He wouldn't let me console him. Indeed, this man loved animals, more, in fact, than he cared for me, or for himself, or for any other human in the world, except perhaps his mother.

When he doesn't know I'm watching, the man I love now is so sweet to our new dog that I think my heart will whistle so loud it will give me away. Four years ago, I never thought I'd see the day. Over Thanksgiving, when we lost our pit bull Kimber, I think he wanted to cry, though I never saw him do it if he did. At its worst, sorrow can destroy a man. At its best, sorrow will show us who we are, who we can be.

As for me, I will always be an animalero. Ever since I was a boy. Dogs, cats, owls and other pajaritos, jaguars and ocelots, wolves, coyotes, and armadillos, of course, and, of course, los tlaquaches. But dogs, especially dogs—I feel most at ease when I am home with my family of dogs—I don't know how else to say this. Perhaps this is my pack, perhaps I, too, simply yearn to belong.

vi.

When you are a boy, you also might have a pack. As part of a pack, you also have the choice to go along with shit or to eschew it. When you are a boy, so often, it is true: the world is yours. When you are a brown boy, the world is and is not yours. A queer boy, too. We are told this in so many, many ways. And so, it is, in fact, routinely easier to go along with racist shit, to laugh at rape jokes, to join in or silently acquiesce as people are ridiculed as faggots or illegals. But these beliefs are not yours. No. None of us owned this shit. Not when we were born, not when our skin first tasted air, not at the moment of our first scream. It was given to us, placed over our bodies like a heavy coat of sticker burrs and tar, forced upon us, even. Eventually, though, we make it ours. We choose. If we don't molt that tar-burr coat given to us by the world, if we don't cut away those patches of shit clinging to our hands and our chests, then, we accept those burrs. Accepting them means we are okay with these violences enacted upon others. And often, and tragically, enacting these violences is a way to say we belong, that we are members of the pack. Yes, we choose the kind of boys, the kinds of men we become. Or if, even, we don't become men at all. At some point in our lives, gradually. All of us. Molting, choosing, tar, chest, power and burrs.

vii.

If I tell you I once believed only good men deserve love, what will I say next? If I tell you this is an old story, a story older than fire and bloodshed, will you believe me?

viii.

Perhaps it is the fact tlaquaches are maligned for their queerness, for that pouch they shouldn't have or use, for their semblance to other dismissed animals like rats, that we carry aversions to them. "They are so fucking ugly," someone told me once. "So gross."

I will not try to explain away others' disgust for these animals as much as I will try to convey the idea that ugliness is a variable, and the truest discoveries in life also live in the realm of generalizations and variables.

Once, years ago, when I first moved to San Antonio, I bought a camera, and one night sitting on my stoop, I watched a tlaquache make its way out of the alley across my caliche driveway in front of my second truck to the landing below the stairs—a small, square, concrete patch, where I threw food for the stray cats who lived around my house. I watched the little animal eat. I watched it move slowly, watchful and weary at first, and then eat more profoundly, swallowing the morsels as if, in fact, the creature knew pleasure and comfort and wanted joy to last. I tried one night to capture the not-so-small tlaquache with my new camera. I waited by the house. The porchlight dim; my camera on a tripod; my little dog asleep inside. Back then, I did not know much about lighting or shutter speeds and apertures, so when I clicked the trigger, the animal froze and then as I tried to adjust the focus again, the noise startled the animal who took off, leaving its meal behind, abandoning its joy, abandoning it for safety—swiftly, he scurried beneath and then behind my truck and back into the overgrown alley.

ix.

When I was 12, I watched my mom's boyfriend and his friends beat the shit out of a opossum with a baseball bat. Maybe I was 13. Maybe I was one of them, maybe I am a lie.

x.

And so, it is an old story. Older perhaps than story itself. The boy and the men. The boy and weapons. The boy on the hunt. The boy and the expectations, the duties he will fill. The boy on the farm, in the field. The boy standing before the great sky, the darkness of trees, the wide expanse of his breath, the one inside him, the one he is putting out into the great world. But the boy who isn't what a boy is supposed to be and be and mean. But the boy who doesn't want blood on his knuckles–not in his teeth, not on his clothes, not on the ideas that make themselves swirl in his head like a clutch of starlings. Not at all. Nothing like that.

xi.

Like a thread. I heard it one night, as I lay in bed, my arm pressed against my husband's chest, my arm harboring the soft pull and tug of his lungs—that reminder that something inside him meant there was something also inside of me that moved, even when my eyes shut, when I forgot I was living and fell deeply or not-so-deeply into my sleep.

We lay there, my husband and me, and the dogs lay beside us, the big mastiff by my side of the bed, her snoring wakeful and overblown, and beside my husband, on the other side of the room, the boxer mix we'd rescued a few months before, after our pit bull died unexpectedly one night and the house felt emptier than it had in a very long time. Each night now, my husband and I lie like this, and sometimes, the house is as quiet as a thumb; sometimes, it is quieter, a noiselessness that echoes an impossible silence so near the center of San Antonio, the city where we live. But one night, I heard that thread. In the other room, across the hall, that long thin hair of a noise. The boy boxer stood up, and I could see his thick shadow at the doorway, his ears up and opened, and he looked back at me, asking, *Do you hear that, too?*

Long ago, I feared being the only one awake in the house. I can tell you those reasons, but first I have to explain them to myself.

I think it was the boxer mix, Sweet Baby Ray, the rescue group named him, who first heard the baby tlaquache who'd entered our house. It isn't hard for me to hear the dogs get up in the middle of the night (when I was a child, I listened for people moving around the house, the trailer, the apartment, at night—perhaps you know what that is like, listening for doom, hoping it wasn't coming, but knowing well it could, and would, like it had before, come to you, to others you loved, gripping bedsheets like they were your tongue or the wind inside your bones, all the while knowing this wasn't life but it was yours—and if you know this, then, for that, I am sorry).

And I didn't know, not at first, that it was, in fact, a small tlaquache who'd somehow made his way down the hall, but he found himself in or led himself, maybe (allowing him more volition), into the laundry room, where I used to feed the small hairless dog we called Tiny, back when he was still alive. (Blind and using only his three good legs, Tiny ate separated from the other, bigger dogs, so that he could eat his fill unbothered, and frequently, he ate to his belly's content, leaving only a few morsels of kibble in his bowl or beside it.) I imagine when the baby tlaquache tiptoed his way through our house, he'd caught the scent of Iams, and I say this because I don't know about the capabilities of an opossums' sense of scent, so I only imagine, like I only can imagine my heart beating with something like a starling—one of them, separated from the rest of the clutch, as they dance, as they move along, as they leave to some place better than before.

I haven't ever enjoyed being the only one awake in the house, especially not when I was young, but that night with the little tlaquache in the laundry room, I was glad it was only me, as I don't know exactly how my husband would have taken the sight of the little uninvited animal in our house, holding a morsel of kibble in his two tiny paws, eating and eating and just across from our bedroom.

And soon, I could hear it, too. The sound of teeth breaking into a morsel. Sound of chewing. Sound of a sound I didn't want to hear while the whole house stood without light.

It took me no time to jump out of bed, and I found it in the laundry room, behind the grey mop bucket, in a corner, near the bowl where the blind hairless dog we called Tiny took his dinner every night. From the laundry room door, the boy boxer stared at the small animal.

I remember thinking, *James is going to freak.*

I remember Baby Ray looking up at me like, *What should I do, dad? Do I get him? Dad, can I?*

xii.

Each of us decides, a decision already made before us.

"It's the way of the world," a man I met outside a bar told me one night, seeing my sadness, as we drove to his apartment, my hand in his lap, and a doe, dead on the side of the road.

But is it, really? The world's way—or ours? *Isn't life what we make of it?* I thought, as his big body lay on top of mine, as his breath gnawed at my chest and he asked me to tell him the story of all my tattoos. Easily, I could whisper those stories, all of them, pushing my rosary and spider webs and the name on my neck deep into his chest hair, into his breath made of Listerine and cigars and loneliness, but I couldn't stop thinking of that deer beside the road. But even with the dead deer on my mind, I let him kiss me, and I couldn't tell you the rest, as I can barely recall it now, all these years after those facts.

It's the way the world works, que no?

The forgetting, the dying, the deciding.

Yes, we decide to do with the world or it does with us. What that decision does inside our bodies, in our soft mouths and our even softer lungs, in the small territories of the soft heart and the crawl space underneath its soft meat?

xiii.

Because all of my life, I have been accused of being a man who is too sensitive. Because perhaps I am too full of the milk of human kindness. Because perhaps I wear it in my beard or underneath it, perhaps on my brown skin, inside my tattoos of eagles and praying hands, of saguaro corazones and other men's names. Because softness is a trait not every man will openly wield. Because there's a price to wearing softness. Because whomever you are, there is a consequence squatting beside your softness, a declaration, a truth, a pillar of lies, a crack made of river water and salt. Because there's a cost to letting your maleness fur with its mottles and its marks, its coat made of cariño and mystery and vulnerability and longing and suffering, joy. Because softness is not muted, and softness screams its name as if the name was bone and dry soil and all the unwanted and wished-dead things moved by wind. Because a body is never just a body. Because softness is the body, but softness is also the breath of holiness inside each of us, which is love of life, which is an awareness that people and things outside of ourselves do matter, which means connectedness, and which, if you are like me, means God.

xiv.

As I flipped on the laundry room light, I worried the boy boxer might go for the creature, having already killed an opossum on our patio one night.

(A small thing, I found her near the steps, her fur damp and matted and slobbery from where my dog had taken her small body into his mouth. So tiny, like a kitten, I recall thinking as I picked up her limp figure and set her on a white cotton towel in a box. I remembered the dog's mouth frothy, a foam formed around his muzzle. And I'd like, now, to think he didn't know what he was doing, that in him there isn't a killswitch, a blood-hunger waiting to ignite, some inherent tendency that propelled him to take her small body into his teeth, squeeze down, and shake, but perhaps that absence of instinct is even more terrifying. As much as I say I am an animalero, there is so much about the animals around me I don't know. I suppose on most days I am okay living without touching their secrets. With heaviness in my mouth, I set the little tlaquache's box by a tree in the front yard, and I stepped away, hoping the idea of living was more than an abstraction, that it had more traction than a sigh, more mass than the simplest of all hopes. In the morning, she had stiffened. I'd feared this likelihood like a tree branch, like a gust, like a hole underneath our house, whispered. And while I had hoped really to find an empty box, I walked out into the yard wearing only my sleeping shorts and stoicism. I'd locked the dogs in the house. Whining that they wanted out, the two big dogs watched. And I stood beside the tree, holding my own hands, looking at lifelessness, at consequence, at her.)

With the small tlaquache eating kibble in front of our washing machine, I put the boy dog in the bedroom and shut the door, and this woke my husband, so I told him, "Keep Baby Boy inside. There's something in the house." I tried first with a wicker basket to corral the small opossum, and I also had a towel to throw over him, an approach I learned from my second lover when he rescued a skunk—if you cover them in darkness, they might not fight you.

But the small opossum, with its small opposable thumbs, quickly made his way out of the braided container, and before I could get the bath towel around him, he rushed down the hall, under a door to one of the spare bedrooms, and under the closet door.

Opening the closet door, trying to grab the baby opossum with the towel, he hissed, and at this point, I had to ask my husband for help. The small guy shit himself in the closet, the fear on his body; I don't know if opossums can see possibilities, potentialities, but I know that he saw me and he saw my bigger hands and my husband standing behind me, holding a flashlight. I don't need to imagine his terror. I can still hear him hissing.

In the end, we used a red plastic bucket, and I walked the little guy outside, as the boy boxer stood at the side door wanting to follow me. I imagine those moments in that bucket—the small opossum may have lived panic and perhaps confusion, a feeling of being trapped. Perhaps, too, he understood danger, clawing against the red sides, sliding down, unable to grab hold of anything that might lead to a way out.

That night, I let him go near a tree in my front yard.

xv.

I've known this for a very long time: Some of us let monsters into our houses. If they come, we let them stay. Sometimes, they knock. They might wear politeness and civility on their faces. Maybe they place themselves in our lives strategically, grooming us, grooming out our distrust, giving themselves good light. Our mothers let them in, our fathers, too. And if your mother or father or grandfather or some other family member is that monster, does that mean God let them in? Eventually, when we begin to see what or who they are, we may try to send them out, but they come back, even if we block entrances with sofas and books, even if we nail shut all the windows and doors, lock them with muscles and prayer, even if we agree not to tell another living soul.

xvi.

Even shame is a weapon when wielded as such. Which proves that anything can be weaponized. Which proves that anything can be carried around in a pouch, taken out. Anything can be made to bleed.

xvii.

But there is another story, too. An old story. Old, too, like that other story. The story of a boy who does it. The boy who doesn't walk away.

The boy with blood on his hands. The boys who kills. Knuckles, whole fists, measured-and-unmeasured hands that did what boy-hands and boy-bodies are, indeed, told to do. And, after the fact, he might look back, and he might miss home or know wrongness, because he accepts indifference is an indictment of godlessness. This is an old story, too. And this is a long walk home, the long arms, or the short ones, hanging beside the boy's body, dripping with the abstractions of guilt, of confusion, of new consciousness and shifting, dripping with despair, because it is, indeed, a painful thing to live with one's blood deeds. It is a painful thing to walk away from the boys we are supposed to be. Violence will haunt a boy even when he forgets it's there.

xviii.

And I'm going to tell you another story. This is the story of how I am not good. This is the story of contradictions and walls. A story of bricks and opossum bones. This is the story of failing, which is the story, then, of what kind of man I have become and how. Early in my life, I decided that while I didn't know what type of man I would be, I knew the type of man I would not be: vicious, cruel, spiteful, unaware. I wanted to be kind. I wanted to carry compassion in my hands like a kite. The feathers, the talons, the long-sharp beak and eyes. Really, all my life, I have just wanted to be good. Really, all my life, I have worried that I was not good.

xix.

You see, there was an opossum living under our house several years ago. This bothered my husband, and he wanted him out. To appease my husband, I read about ways to distance a tlaquache from the place he or she calls home, which happened, also, simultaneously, to be our home, the one my husband and I moved into that summer when I told my body it was alright to love him.

154

I tried sprinkling cayenne pepper around the crawl space door, red powder staining the concrete. I tried running my dogs around the house, after reading online that dogs' scents can dissuade opossums and skunks, although I'd already tried the cayenne pepper, which seemed to only dissuade the dogs. So then I tried dipping rags in dog urine, which seemed implausible at first, given that my dogs piss in the grass and the earth being the earth does what it does, however, by this point Tiny, the small hairless, had begun eschewing the grass for his business, opting instead for the concrete. It was easier, then, to soak rags in puddles of Tiny's dark yellow piss and lay them out by the entrance to the crawl space. But I admit, as much as I wanted each of these tactics to work, as much as I would have taken any of these solutions, each of them flopped. The opossum would not give up his home, or hers, which also was mine and James's.

When I admitted I'd failed, James suggested we block the entrance.

"We can't trap him in there," I said, after a few moments, judging my own words, harnessing them and not wanting the words that the heaviness in my mouth made to grow sharp or fling out like the jaggedness that was happening inside me.

In certain ways, I was dispirited by the idea of making the opossum leave. And while I didn't expect to fully convince my husband of the benefits of keeping a tlaquache around, I did my best to promote the idea that opossums eat ticks and other bugs and even, I've heard, run off rats. There is nothing deliberate, though, about not wanting to force a creature out of its home—and I say this fully aware that it was because, and only because, it was a tlaquache that I felt guilt wad up inside me like a hive, exterminating any rat I would have said fine to.

But didn't I say all creatures want love? And deserve it?

But didn't I say I wanted to be a good man? Kind and not cruel, conscious of my hands?

xx.
Then, too, there is the origin of *opossum*. The word comes from the early 17th century—from Virginia Algonquian opassom, from op, 'white,' and *assom*, 'dog.'

If my grandmother from Coahuila were still alive today, I might ask her what she knew of the word tlaquache. She would hold her long braid, the ends of its grayness, *and* she'd hold out her hand, which was a reminder of what happens to brownness when it's old, and she might tell me what I already know, which is the word itself is brown, browner than me, brown like aguacate like Tenochtitlan brown like xoloitzcuintlis and tierra and time.

So maybe it's the brownness of the animal I love. So maybe it's the likeness to dogs. Or maybe it's the story. In other words, maybe it's the guilt I will forever carry when I watched and did nothing as my mom's boyfriend and his friends beat the shit out of an opossum with a baseball bat.

xxi.
Someone, right now, is thinking, *It's just a fucking opossum. Just. Just.*

xxii.
Someone, one time, said, *They're just queers and hookers and junkies.* Just.

xxiii.

At this point in my life, I do think my mother's second husband hated me, because he knew I was queer. Do I need to prove it? Of course not. Not my queerness, not his hatred. What's there to document?

I know he hated people like me.

My mother knew he hated people like me. She told us. I think back then my mother knew I was queer, also.

Back then, I think my mother hated us too.

And so, what becomes of one's body when two truths inside you face off? When two things you know to be true, on a collision course, bare their teeth and glare? Who wins? Who do you help? What side do you pick, if not your own?

My mother was lonely. She was lonely for a man.

Perhaps you know that kind of loneliness. I know that in the middle of my years, I do. And so I can understand, now more than halfway through my own life, that sometimes the body will do what it has to do to not be lonely.

But hurt is hurt, and hurt is one of those elements like a rock standing in a yellowing field or a tree branch that's broken off but hangs, still, unable to fully separate from the rest of the tree: joto. Joto.

Joto, if you can hear the bones breaking in another human's mouth, then, you understand, like I understand, like we understand— there is no need to prove shit. No need to pick up the stone smeared with shit and hold it up to the light so others will believe its truth, there in the lines of your palm. No need to climb the broken tree and point to the hinge, no need to grab the splinters, that juncture where togetherness ended its hold on the tree and the forces at work set in.

It's not that hard to know when people hate us.

And after the fact, what else is there to write down or photograph or sing of except the simplicity of hate. He found me ugly. I reminded him of something or someone from who he was before, and he wanted me gone.

I don't need to tell you my mom's second boyfriend, who later became her husband, ran me off. I was twelve, maybe thirteen. He did it with beatings and insults, by killing that opossum, and by wishing me not there, which is the way men often do.

There are stories I am not going to tell you. In any case, we begin to learn this tenet early on in life if we are watching: if we see something as ugly or unworthy, as lesser, then it is easy to allow it to be thrown away, to be uprooted and removed, to be smashed with baseball bats and condemnations, whole fists, silences and vitriol, lies and laws, ultimately destroyed.

We begin by watching others do it, hearing it transpire in our houses, on playgrounds, in locker rooms, when no one is looking and also in full plain sight of those who might put a halt to the torture. And one day, one day, we do it ourselves.

xxiv.

I am willing to concede that none of us is as innocent as we'd like to be.

I am willing to concede that I have hurt other things, other people.

I am willing to concede that there is a luxury and privilege to the act of washing blood from our hands.

Yet, I am not willing to concede the pain of this story. In this sense, I am a man. In this sense, we will always be those boys.

xxv.

In the end, I will tell you that one night, after the gym, my husband and I drove up to our house to find the opossum, just leaving the crawl space, illuminated in the driveway by the headlights of our red Ford. The animal scampered, climbing over our small retaining wall, into the neighbors' dark grass.

James did it quickly. In minutes, he'd walked in darkness back behind the wooden shed, emerging with a few bricks, his hands gripping the stone as if stone itself could be both resolution and broken promise. On a night with the summer overwhelming the air, my husband stacked the bricks in front of the crawl space, and I went into the house to tend to the dogs, to give them their food and cariño, to refill their water. In moments, my husband entered the house—he had blocked the entrance.

What's done was done, and we went to bed, after eating, after watching the late news, and in the morning, we made love, and I made breakfast and I kissed him goodbye before going to work. I figured the little tlaquache would have to find another home. It's just the way things worked, in life, in this life I was making.

But the truth is we didn't know that there was another opossum, thinking that only one of them lived under our house. What happened next is a damn spot on my hands, proof that I have stopped begging stars to hide their fires.

Perhaps I am only making excuses for myself, as men often do. Perhaps I am trying to defend what James and I did, or redefine it, as men often do. But there's no way I could have known another opossum was living beneath our house when we shut off the entrance to the crawl space. Admitting that is fine, though it does nothing to alter the fact there are bones trapped somewhere in the walls of our house.

xxvi.
When the exterminator came, it was because the smell of something dead had permeated half the house. The front half: the living room and the office and the kitchen, the hall by the mantle, the fireplace, and one of the bedrooms. The man wore a blue suit, which he put on, over his clothes, to go under the house. As he crawled under my house, I stared at the inside of the crawl space door—there were scratch marks embedded in the wood, snagged on the splinters there was fur. There before me was what I, what we, had done.

After fifteen or so minutes, the man in the blue suit who was supposed to find the dead thing emerged, although he'd found nothing, except a hole underneath the house, he said, near the big fireplace, that led up into one of the walls.

"We can punch out the walls. To find it," he said.

I asked, "How will you find it?" "We'll just have to start breaking through walls. We could find it the first time. Or we could go through all the walls."

Somewhere a tlaquache had died in our house. I thought of that desperation, of trying to escape a house that wouldn't let you out. When he, or she, died, what was I doing? Was I lying on the floor, playing with my dogs, whispering sweetnesses to them, stroking their long necks or their bellies? Was I reading the book I was rereading at the time, Anne Carson's *Autobiography of Red,* or writing some draft of a shitty poem I was trying to make good? For all I knew, James and I were opening each other up as the small animal took its last breaths, as it suffered and struggled and finally surrendered to death. For all I knew, I was feeling sorry for myself or looking at the parts of my body I don't like in a mirror when it died. I don't know. I don't.

In the end, we did not punch through the walls.

"It will go away after a few days. Three or four of them," the man in the blue suit who'd been under my house said.

As a result, I hung bags of charcoal in all of the rooms. On doorknobs and in closets I hung coal. I found them at Lowe's, near the rat traps and/or the air filters, I can't remember exactly. I sprayed aerosols, but the combination of rot and cinnamon fucked with my head. Even tobacco leaf candles and boiling orange rind did little to quell the air. And for a few days I watched the dogs sniff urgently at the house. The mastiff sometimes pawed at the floor, and I wondered if there were other things living under my house, trying to get out. Every so often, I caught a whiff, and in time, I removed the bricks and let the door again be moved.

xxvii.

But hurt is hurt, and we each carry it around. Some days, we pass
it off or around; and too often we aren't even aware that we're pushing
our hurt off onto someone, asking or telling and perhaps, tragically,
even forcing someone else to carry it.

xxviii.

Splinters and lightning and the echoes of things that, over all of these
years, have stuck to our skin and our bones and our hair— alley or
monte or room or field, crawl space, or inside the walls of us, maybe
a red bucket, maybe a box, maybe a backyard under a streetlamp by a
fence, maybe a pouch that has grown inside us. The world is what we
make of it, que no?

xxix.

The truth is I was glad when my mother's second husband left
her. Or when she left him (even all these years later, I don't know
which version of the story is truer). I understand now that to him, like
to millions of others, my queerness, our queerness is monstrous and
therein must be displaced, interrupted, destroyed.

In Carson's book, Heracles loves the monster Geryon. Or more
accurately the other way around—the monster Geryon loves Heracles,
who is cruel, who will be the monster's good death, his pain, his one
volcanic memory.

I admit there are times in my life when I pursued monsters, when I
loved them and thought I could save them. From themselves, from the
world, from me.

All creatures want love. I believe that. I will say it. Again and again.

I don't think tlaquaches are monstrous at all. I am enamored with images of mama tlaquaches carrying pups atop their backs, traveling, taking them all. I am enamored with the idea of the pouch they are not supposed to have. Or we.

To someone, right now, I am monstrous for what I just said, for what my husband and I unknowingly and knowingly did to the tlaquache beneath our house. Some days I can be washing dishes or sweeping up the dog hair, and I remember there are tlaquache bones embedded somewhere in our walls, and then, I believe I am monstrous.

To someone, when I hold my husband tonight, when we lay in our bed and I turn off the lights and I press my brownness against his body, that will be especially monstrous. (I hope you and your loved one(s) are partaking in that monstrosity too.)

The pockets of men are monstrous, also, to some. The pockets of women are monstrous to others. The pockets of those of us who are they—their pockets, also, especially, now, in these times, are seen as monstrous by some and are under attack.

It's not that hard for others to know when we hate them. It's not that hard to know when we are hated, or when we hate ourselves.

But even monsters can be missed; even the monstrous can be yearned for. I suppose some days I have to remind myself that all creatures deserve love, deserve affection—including myself, including the parts of me and the memories I don't love. I suppose sometimes I have to remind myself that all of the world is stark naked, it is, at some point, when no one or when everyone is watching what we do.

Originally published in our Fall 2018 issue, *Edges*

PINTO ("PENIS" & SLANG FOR "CHICK" IN BRAZILIAN PORTUGUESE)

Lucas de Lima

if the dream is to go beyond empire

if the dream is to stretch our extremities

all the way thru

if o poder emana do povo

& the people's emanations

refuse to be privatized

what does it mean that i fisted pinto

& became a chicken

what does it mean that pinto opened my hole

without extracting my soul

Lucas de Lima on "Pinto"

What inspired this piece?

This poem was recently published in my book *Tropical Sacrifice*, which is a wishbone against a fascist heart/a prophetic, dream-filled narrative based on the spiritual journey of a chicken. Used for sacrificial ritual in Afro-Brazilian religion, the chicken becomes a re-enchantment of the poet's ancestry. Her superior vision gives access to histories of genocide and ecocide, opening a portal to Indigenous, Afro-diasporic, queer and nonhuman worlds. From the favela to the Amazon to the astral plane, it is the half-winged bird who escapes the factory farm, inviting voices to bleed out of the sky.

Originally published in our Fall 2018 issue, *Edges*

Soft Bodies

Nicole Callihan

While sweeping the carcasses of ladybugs into a blue dust pail, I think of how it might be a good idea to build soft bodies around robots, or of how I might use my own soft body to surround a good, patient robot who has only mechanical desires. I could donate the flesh of my thighs and the pulp of my lungs, and seeing this robot on the street, you might think she is me, and maybe you would speed up because you remember that terrible thing I did three falls ago, or maybe you would slow down, because, twice, I was nice at drop-off. I would like to feel oil slowly poured into my ear. My student says that if we can offer robots to the ill and infirm no one will have bed sores, and my Facebook feed says that my dad's stepmother died several days ago, and yesterday, taking Eva for braces, I thought it would be easier if her teeth were constructed out of manmade materials and would, thus, already be straight. There are buttons on my back which can be pressed to make me audibly moan. For what I am hardwired, I cannot say.

Nicole Callihan on "Soft Bodies"

Reading this piece again, what reflections do you have?

Each winter, dozens and dozens of ladybugs come to die in a little corner of my home. Their bright, hard-shelled bodies knocking into my dust pail must've made me think of soft bodies, and—as it was mid-semester—I must've been puzzling through the ethics of human-robot interaction with my students. What does it mean to be mechanized? What algorithms of language and domesticity and bureaucracy are we already following? How have I come to learn of the death of a loved one from a newsfeed? What is this spot on my back which you have touched to make me audibly moan? As we move deeper and deeper (*shallower and shallower?*) into our relationships with our tiny handheld computers, there will be much with which to reckon.

sent from (& w/ & by) my iPhone

Originally published in June 2018 online at asterixjournal.com
Selected for *BEST OF THE NET*

My Big Gay Essay

Carley Moore

1.

When I was sixteen, my best friend and I found a bolt of bright, mustard yellow, polyester fabric in the clearance bin at Joanne Fabrics. We wanted to make wide-legged high-waisted pants—like I now see when I scan the racks at Top Shop—and long hip-hugging skirts. Neither of us had mastered zippers, but we were fine with an elasticized waistband. But it was the color that really got us. Nobody in our dying Rust Belt town wore this color. It was obnoxious and loud, not to be missed against the gray, dirt snow. We bought the whole bolt for maybe five bucks.

The fabric was so thick it jammed our sewing machines, but we re-threaded the needles and made two hideous pairs of big-legged pants. The waistbands were bunchy and uncomfortable because the elastic was big and also from the clearance bin. No matter. We loved them and wore them to school. Our few punk friends marveled at our DIY skills, while we withstood the usual attacks from football players and cheerleaders. Whispers and looks. Not like the beatings our male friends endured. The pants were uncomfortably hot because they were made of tires and plastics or whatever stew of pesticides and polymers made up 80s polyesters. If there were a fire, we'd have been burned alive by our pants. One of us may have gotten a yeast infection from wearing them.

We were living a fantasy version of ourselves. We needed to believe we could make something out of nothing. That the ugly could become noteworthy and that we could turn garbage into couture. We didn't follow style rules. We made our own. We wanted to feel yellow—bright, futuristic, loud, while our town regularly told us that we were dirt.

One of the many brilliant threads in Andrea Lawlor's new novel, *Paul Takes the Form of a Mortal Girl*, is around the rituals of clothing—their power, their possibility for subversion, their ability to transform us, and the way they situate and complicate our genders. Paul, who has a kind of superpower, and can transform his body into a woman's body (with a spongy vagina) and sometimes a more masculine male body (with a bigger penis), has a talent for clothing and fantasy among other less bankable skills. In the middle of the novel, Paul moves to San Francisco to recover from a break-up in Provincetown, where he lived as Polly for several months. The narrator admits:

> Paul had to have a job. But maybe not drag. He walked and listed his other known talents: pouring beer without too much head, shoplifting, washing dishes, organizing items, knowing what was going to fashionable a little bit early, thrifting, clever commentary, introducing people to other people, cutting pictures out of magazines with x-acto knives, knowing when people where open to having sex, having sex, being gay. (227)

I still count some of these things as my talents, and still one has to have a job. Sigh. I don't want to give too much of the novel away, but Lawlor is so deft at recreating that early nineties, Generation X, slacker, queer, state school milieu, that I fell nostalgically back into the time where I spent hours pulling together an outfit for a party, took the campus bus everywhere, and held several different jobs while trying to cobble together my $150 a month rent. And yet the novel is futuristic and almost sci-fi in its ideas about gender—as mutable, as ever changing, and a physicality we can mostly control at will with our minds.

2.

My dad's favorite movie is Blade Runner. I like to joke with my therapist that I'm a replicant, your basic pleasure model. I find this comforting, and my neurological disorder often leaves me with joint pain that makes me feel robotic and spastic. My father raised my brother and I to believe we were part of a special tribe, that there is nobody else like us. Misunderstood smarties. Robots. Replicants. Aliens to our own planet.

To be raised by a narcissist father is to learn quickly how to mirror and please. My father has always liked me best when I am staring into his face, nodding along with his story, and not saying a word. Growing up, he liked to play full albums for my brother and I while we sat trapped on the couch. Sometimes they were amazing—my father introduced me to Prince, R.E.M., Steely Dan, The Pretenders, The Talking Heads, and Z.Z. Top. There was also Molly Hatchett, A.C.D.C, and Metallica. Once, while a born-again Christian family improbably ate dinner at our atheist table, my father insisted on playing "Darling Nicki."

The mother of that family, whose daughter had shunned me at a Christian sleepaway camp I attended in a lame middle-school attempt to try new things, turned to me, with a sweetly evil smile and said, "Do you like this song?"

"I love Prince," I might have said while my mother yelled, "They hate it. Turn it off!"

We were having one of our torture dinners. No matter the guests or if it was just us, we couldn't get along. My father, genuinely believed he could convert these bland white Christians into liking Prince. He thought if they could just listen, really listen, they'd get it. It was always like that with him. Pay attention. Stick with me. It will all make sense.

When my ex-husband and I separated, my father lamented, "But how will I see him?" A couple weeks later he accused me of "being gay and ruining my marriage." A couple months later, I decided to stop talking to him.

Oh shut up Dad, I wanted to say to him, *There are so many ways to ruin a marriage.*

3.

Earlier in *Paul Takes the Form of a Mortal Girl,* Paul as Polly sits in a cafe with their girlfriend Diane in Provincetown. Diane wants to help set free an abused dog and is annoyed with Polly for lacking focus:

> Paul looked down at his burgundy cords, his black Runways tee shirt (a church thrift shop score in Orleans—how jealous would Jane be) tight over his waffled long-john shirt, his Save the Whales! belt buckle with its fresco humpback. He liked this new look, enjoyed this foray into androgynous style, liked the little fuck-you shadows of femininity he deployed. He wasn't trying to copy Diane, but he did like them to be complementary. He did manage to find a copy of Times Square at City Video and rented it for them to watch together, had tried to explain to her his thoughts on runaway tomboy rocker dyke gender, but she'd been unimpressed. Diane didn't like to talk about gayness very often. Paul estimated that he held back two out of five gay-themed comments. (201)

Androgynous style. The little fuck you shadows of femininity. Deployment and subterfuge. Hiding in plain sight. I've long used clothing to confuse myself, to confuse others, to register as unreadable or misplaced. I've been happiest at 21 and now in my mid-forties with short boyish hair. Baggy boyish clothes delight me, but I'm often in dresses that are technically inappropriate for the occasion. I sometimes teach in a silver sequined dress because it cheers me up. I wear yoga pants everywhere. I use a jean jacket as a suit coat. I wear bikinis to show my stretch marks. I hate seeing fellow moms in beach dresses, though I totally get the desire to cover up. The truth is, I don't often see myself. Can we ever really see ourselves from the outside? Our asses especially? The backs of our necks? There is the image we think we give off and something far more complicated that gets transmitted to the world.

There was that leather/pleather leaf print tie-dyed jacket I bought in Albany with Janna. A neon green and black mini-skirt from Betsy Johnson, a $15 Century 21 score. A mint green lozenge of a dress, stitched on a machine like my mother used to make us matching yellow lace wedding dresses. Those purple and black combat boots, faux Fluevog. I wore those to book Writing Center appointments, meet drunks at Sophie's and Mars Bars, and to lie across laps in the backseats of cabs. The TJ Max bras I buy with Stef and the drawstring skirt my daughter and I stitched for Genevieve the rabbit.

When I used the gender conversion app on Facebook, the only thing it adds is stubble. I feel this is another hint for me, that I'm circling something I need to figure out.

"But you only write about your relationships with men," my friend is pushing me at a bar. She's femme, identifies as a lesbian, and is a truth teller. I take it in because listening is something I can do.

"That's true," I admit. "This is new to me. I haven't been in a relationship with a woman. I make out with them, I'm attracted to them, but I want to do more, and I need to write about it."

There is more to this conversation. Another good friend is there too. We are talking about openness, tenderness, risks, and dogs.

We are talking about a woman I met two weeks ago at a poetry reading. We wandered around together with a small crowd afterwards. She stayed close to me, said things like, *You know where to go.*

Everyone left. We had the dim divey back room of the bar to ourselves. We were magnetized. Mouths. Lips. Hands. I slid my hands under her shirt, rubbed at her jeans. She put her hands down my pants. I was wearing period underwear, which is like a chastity belt. I felt an ideological wall falling down. I am a Gemini and we can be sloppy with our love. I had some tequila. What is gender? What is a dick or a man anyway? My whole life I've been taking care of dicks, petting, sucking, rubbing them and maybe I don't have to all of the time? Maybe it's not about gender at all, but people, a person. I sound like I haven't read any theory on anything, but I've read it all. I should quote Butler, Sedgewick, Preciado, or Halberstam, but I'm not feeling it. I've got Lawlor. They are my theory. The novel is theory at its most embodied form I think. I'm not a person who "hates labels," and I'm not trying to be dodgy. I'm confused sometimes. I hate binaries. I am often two or three things at once. I'm queer. Bisexual. There I wrote it. If anything I think too much, and suffer from deep earnestness.

We stumbled out of that bar. We ate pizza and stared out the window at the stupid, gentrifying East Village. We kept touching each other. We talked about another woman we both have a crush on, a mutual friend who confused us. I told her about my boyfriend. She told me about her wife. We love them both very much. We talked about our rules for openness. We didn't improbably go home together.

4.

There's something very silly about coming out at 45. I mean, like, who cares? I find myself back in my state school town, like Paul in Lawlor's novel, feeling nostalgic for all my gay best boyfriends and their coming out to me. My response was often, "I know and it's great and I love you." But I shouldn't have said "I know," because it takes away the drama of it, the declaration, the announcement that felt so important in the 90s and maybe still does.

I tell my mother on the phone and she says, "I'm not surprised."

"How come?" I ask.

"Because you like to go to Long Island with S and D," as if traveling with a queer couple means anything in particular.

"And you can't live here." She's referring to the dying gray dirt town I left but where everyone in my family still lives. My dear mom, who is always looking for reasons to explain why I left her, why I had to move away to the big city and live such a precarious life.

"But mom," I tease, "That's not why I can't live there. I mean I feel like a big dyke when I'm home. I don't look like anyone else, they stare. It's bad there. There are no jobs there for me, no thing I can do. It's so small, I'd suffocate."

"Everybody stares here," she's been saying this to me my whole life. In my teens and twenties, it drove me crazy. It felt like an excuse, a cop out. But now I find it cute. My mom is 70. Like most of the women in her family, she is improbably healthy. Tough. Fit. Totally with it mentally.

I don't want anything to happen to her. I want us to know each other as fully as possible. We've come a long way in our relationship.

"It's okay," she says.

"I know."

And then she starts telling me about the weather and a book she's reading.

5.

During the first year of my marriage to a man, who is now my ex-husband, dear friend and the father of my child, I wandered around the yellowed, gilded streets of Florence. I was lucky to be there! I was teaching in Tuscany! Everyone told me so! But I was profoundly lonely. I didn't speak Italian. I had no interest in the Renaissance, though I would learn to love David's muscled ass and Fra Angelico's dreamy frescos in their cold monk's cells. I liked to visit Fra Savonarola's hair shirt—a slab of soft leather affixed with porcupine quills. I visited it often to stare at its painful beauty. It wasn't anything like a shirt. More like a belt or a brace. I used to wear leg braces. I hated them, but this was an object of choice. I never consented to those braces which later deformed my feet. I could choose to wear a hair shirt. There was also a self-flagellation stick. A small wooden rod with a tiny whip affixed to the end of it. I coveted that hair shirt because I wanted to feel something instead of sadness. I wanted it to hurt me in the ways I have since wanted my doms to hurt me. I wanted to be under its control so I wouldn't have to think or do anything.

What hurt me most in Florence was that I had no friends. I had gone from a huge circle of loving friends to knowing no one except my husband. He was good company, but he wasn't enough. I had never learned how to be alone. Now I know but it took a divorce and a lot of therapy to just appreciate solitude and not panic. Eventually, I made a friend. An American who had fallen in love with an older Italian man. I would have been miserable without her.

Later, when I came back to Brooklyn, I still had that same feeling. An emptiness. A longing for something I couldn't name. I thought I wanted a baby. I did. Eventually, after a whole bunch of medicine and loss, I had her. She changed my life, made me want to get better, and there is no one I love more in this world, but she didn't fill that hole. No person can fill the kind of hole I'm writing about here.

I still wandered around Brooklyn feeling lost. Waiting for something to happen. The wind on street corners whipping through my then mom bob. The stroller catching on the lip of the curb. The feeling that I was always playing a part very badly, especially at certain playdates with very straight moms who lived in beautiful apartments I would never be able to afford. I didn't want to talk about nursing or baby clothes or my husband's accomplishments. I wanted to talk about bad thoughts and books that did not sell a lot of copies and sex or not sex. I found some moms like me. It took a while. Most of them were poets.

6.

A vagina is a hole to put things into. A pussy is a hole. Hole is a band I still love. There is a book by Maurice Sendak that my kid and I loved called *A Hole is To Dig*. This is the part of the essay where I would like to riff and free associate. It's a place for you to get lost with me the writer. It's a tidal pool or a portal. Maybe it's just distraction or play. The poet in me. Puns. Do you remember a store on lower Broadway called Wholesale Liquidators? They had everything. Forks. Clock radios. Shoes. Now we are stuck with Whole Foods, when really everything we do is piece work. I don't know how to make the parts into a whole. Holy moly. I miss the voice I used to read to my kid when she was really little. It was like many puppet voices. I mostly only use it on cats now. Pussies. Isn't that what sent Earnest Hemingway screaming away from Paris? Gertrude calling to Alice, "Here pussy, pussy, pussy?"

I have wanted more than anything in my life to be my whole self, however complicated and messy that may seem to my family or my partners, but mostly I have not been able to locate my selves or I have hidden them so deep that when they emerge I'm surprised.

I met her six weeks ago. Since I started working on this essay, my boyfriend has left me or maybe I made it so unbearable for him that he had to go. Maybe we are taking a break. Maybe we are okay. Maybe I forgot that I wanted to be free and I lost my way. Maybe I like exploding safe things in Rom Com high drama style. In my experiences with them, cis gendered straight men do a lot of crazy shit. They stop talking. They lie. They threaten to kill themselves. They disappear. They ghost. They pretend everything is okay. They gaslight. Maybe women do all of that too.

I never wrote about him because I sensed he did not want me to.

I texted my brother and mother about my boyfriend leaving and my brother, ever my loving foil, texted, "You can't have two guys, two girls, or a guy and a girl. All illegal moves. Good try though. Flew too close to the sun." I lol.

I sent them a Selena Gomez shrug/smile meme and then we started to text about the kids.

I like that I am the Icarus of my family, the weirdo artist with some crazy escape plan, but I'm not trying to die. Still, I am grateful to their love and humor around my coming out. It has given me strength.

A few weeks earlier I came out to my brother in a text. He texted back, "No worries, Nibbs (his nickname for me since we were kids). I kind of knew a little. I love you always."

I am a quick study. I learn to use my mouth. There is a magical toy. Later it's mostly my hand. The next day my arm quivers and my thighs are weak from exertion. One time when she comes, she punches herself by accident and sees stars. I open and close my thighs. Again and again and again. *Our bodies fit together perfectly*, I think, *because there is no dick in the way.*

Meanwhile I am reading some books. One is the self-help classic *Co-Dependent No More* by Melanie Beatty and the other is Michelle Tea's amazing new collection of essays, *Against Memoir*. In one of my favorite essays is, "On *Chelsea Girls*" which is love letter to Eileen Myles and their determination to tell their own lesbian, working class story, "just my part" (56). Tea writes about reading *Chelsea Girls* and lesbian sex and her own young curiosity about it:

> However, the secret is, everyone, especially perhaps lesbians, must learn to have sex, must teach themselves and one another, constantly

charging up against the limitations of assumption and convention and imagination, not to mention the body. (51)

And later:

> Queer sex could feel like children's make believe and a carnival haunted house and a lion devouring an antelope. It could feel like psychic surgery and a new-fangled workout routine and an aggressive cuddle fest. (52)

I was underlining the book furiously as I read, partly because I was lucky enough to get to interview Tea, so I wanted to take good notes, but I was also reading this book, the way I read many favorite writers, as spirit guides, as self-help, and because I desperately needed some instructions. I did have to learn to have sex with her. We had to teach each other, I had to imagine a new world for myself, and it was like everything Tea described, and more because each body has its own landscapes, smells, wounds, birthmarks, and pleasures regardless of gender. And to calm me down, she kept whispering, "Don't worry. We're just bodies."

7.

I missed him and I cried all night. We spoke on the phone. I was afraid and then I fell asleep. I woke up and watched Janelle Monae's "Emotion Picture," *Dirty Computers* and cried some more. Recognition. Love. Pleasure. The white police state with its whirring insect-like police bugs. The white state in which I reap enormous benefit and am mostly safe, except for when I stand up with my feminist sisters of color and get yelled at or sued or told to shut up, mostly by other white people. But I am never arrested. I am never chased. I am never harassed by the whirring drones. I am never shot.

I am so grateful to Monae for coming out, though she is eclipsing my coming out in every way. Lol. Bisexual. Queer. Pansexual. I am so grateful for this new language from radicals who are younger than me. It's more complicated. I need it.

I think of some of my favorite lines from Gloria Anzaldua's, groundbreaking essay "La Conciencia de la Mestiza: Toward a New Consciousness which I first read as an undergraduate. It spoke to the mix (Swedish, Cuban, German, English, French) in me and still does though I recognize it as utopian. Though aren't all consciousness changing texts? Anzaldua argues, "As a mestiza I have no country, my homeland cast me out; yet all countries are mine because I am every woman's sister or potential lover" (389). I want this to be true. She wrote it in 1987, but for me I know it would be a reach, a grab I can't make. Still, utopias. Sigh.

I see a bit of this mestiza consciousness in *Dirty Computers*. In much of the movie, Monae's character has a boyfriend and a girlfriend. She crosses several landscapes simultaneously and claims futuristic countries as her own.

And some lyrics just stick in my head, like the dirty computer I am. Like the robot, replicant, I was raised and not raised to be.

> *Pink, like the secrets you hide.*
> *I want a crazy, classic life.*
> *Your code is programmed not to love me.*

8.

The day before, I dropped my kid off at school and walked under a crane. It was blocking the street and about to heft something out of a gutted soon-to-be-renovated billion-dollar townhouse. I stopped to watch. I hate cranes—for a couple of years in NYC, they kept falling on people—but I was curious. What was this house's secret? What would I get to see? A man joined me. He was dressed nicely, but barefoot. He had the look of someone on edge, manic. Going shoeless in New York is a particular choice. Still, he stood next to me, calm. We waited. The crane slowly pulled its long arm out of the shell of the house to reveal. Wait. For. It. A tangle of wires and cords. The electric lint ball of the house maybe. A tumbleweed of nothing. I sighed and walked away. I'd wanted treasure—an old piano, a faded rose-colored couch from the 1920s, a claw-foot tub. I wanted the crane to unearth a secret. But there wasn't one.

Carley Moore on "My Big Gay Essay"

Reading this piece again, what reflections do you have?

I wrote this essay as I was coming out to my friends and family that I was bisexual/pansexual, although now I would likely just say as queer. It was a time of incredible upheaval in my life--my boyfriend at the time who I loved very much left me, and I fell in love with a woman for the first time. After a few months, she would be gone from my life too. Because I've always been a part of queer spaces and most of my life, my closest people have been queer, I mistakenly assumed that coming out would be an adventure, something fun and necessary, a final truth to my life. A missing key I suppose. None of my community or friends had experienced this, so I was definitely either not paying attention or willing myself into believing my coming out would be different, but the essay began as a way to hold onto some of that possibility and excitement. Like all of my essays, I was also trying to ask an impossible question and/or solve a problem that I couldn't even name before the writing of the essay. I'm still super proud of this essay and the journey I've been on since it came out: as a queer, nonmonogamous, and disabled person. Coming out at any time is no joke, and coming out late has its own unique challenges and joys. I do sometimes wonder if it was necessary for me to come out in such an explosive, performative way, and wow is biphobia a thing! But that's what I did, so there's no changing it. As for craft, I would say that in my essays, I try to always hold a place for the meta, a moment when I reflect on the making of the essay within the essay itself. I love exposing the seams of the essays--the safety pins that hold it together. Maybe that's the punk in me.

Originally published in our Fall 2020 issue, *The Ferrante Project*

Death of a Family
The Ferrante Project

I.

When did we become mortal enemies? You campaigned early and hard to be our heroine and for a while it worked. But you weren't entertaining any questions. Who besides poets have studied the intimacies of violence and lies? I hear it's cold in heaven and getting colder— inversely proportionate to the warming on earth. The seraphim—bless their souls—are busy burning the documents of the saved. But still no damn heat. You claimed to defy heat like that nineteenth-century Indian princess—she of the silk brocades and stately elephants—who on sultry days teleported herself to the Himalayas.

A good daughter never speaks of the savagery of mothers.

II.

How many did you send? Fifty? One hundred? Thank-you cards to the parents who wish you dead? Subjugation junkie. Holy broken body. There's no end to your tasks. Stop. It's your last moment alive. Then poof, you're gone. What do you say?

III.

Forget your tin scepter. Your baroque concealments. The frail men in your basement bathing hamsters and cooking you colonial meals. Everything around us degrades, sister. Time will steal what remains. Overhead the ex-gods cast their shrinking shadows. No amnesty for the unrepentant, I say. You disagree. We no longer fit in the same life. But in the next one, why not be ordinary sinners together? And I, for one, will speak Polish.

IV.

Soon you'll be dead but I'm done grieving the younger you. Between here and there, then and now, you missed the wild light. Life received you in a thatch hut on stilts. You identified river snakes by their slither and gleam. Peed through the wooden slats into the turbid waters, marking nothing. Because nothing had been taken from you yet. Now your spine crumbles from the unceasing labor of being right. You might live longer without memories but may I remind you of the time you cut my steak into tiny pieces long after I could cut it myself? What's the opposite of a nocturne? A daydream?

Originally published in our Summer 2017 issue,
Kitchen Table Translation

A Lullaby

Kim Hyesoon, translated by Don Mee Choi

Day Thirty Seven

The mother of the child coddled her dead child in her arms.

She sang a lullaby.

This is the contents of her lullaby.

Sleepsleep my baby, die soon so you'll be at ease, so you won't

    have to cry.

The mother of the child dug and buried her child in the middle of her
room.

She also buried her child in the ceiling. Buried in the wall. Buried

in her pupils.

Nobody knew the name of the child's mother but they knew the

    child's name.

Originally published in our Fall 2018 issue, *Edges*

You to the Future

Rosa Alcalá

What would you have said to the future? Future, you will have no scientist in it. Future, your scientist was kissing a Canadian. Future, you could have told me, don't go to his apartment, depress the doorbell for many seconds, wait in his favorite diner around the corner, call him from the dark and humid underground of your last rumbling hope. But, Future, let me tell you something truly remarkable: there were payphones on subway platforms, which was great when you needed one, but if you needed one, things were often not so great. You were late for an interview or you wanted to hear, don't get on that train, I love you, come back to bed. No one on a subway payphone wanted to hear, "Hold on." You were lost, trying to buy weed, calling some guy's beeper. The receiver and keypad were archives of body-cum-city, and in these moments of disorientation, of numbers black and waxy and sticky, the pointer finger brought you closer to your desire with its impeccable memory. Future, I guess you already know that lovers feel their feelings wherever and whatever the mode. On the body, no longer at home. A screen the size of a palm. But in you, Future, no one will know what it's like to make a collect call, to reverse the charges. Or remember the Spanish poet who wrote an ode to his light bulb late one night in the kitchen.

Contributor Bios & Acknowedgments

Rosa Alcalá is a poet and translator from Paterson, NJ. *The New York Times* describes her third and most recent book of poetry *MyOTHER TONGUE* as capturing "the messy emotions and miscommunications that move between languages" and a reminder of "how little precedent there is for honest writing [about mothers and daughters], compared with the epic traditions of fathers and sons." Her poems and translations have appeared in numerous journals, including *Harper's, The Nation, Poetry,* and *American Poetry Review,* as well as in the anthologies *Best American Poetry* (Scribner, 2019 & 21. The recipient of a Foundation for Contemporary Arts Grant to Artists, a National Endowment for the Arts Translation Fellowship, and runner-up for a PEN Translation Award, she is the editor and co-translator of *New & Selected Poems of Cecilia Vicuña* (Kelsey Street Press, 2018). She is currently a Consulting Editor for the University of Chicago Press' Phoenix Poets Series. Her fourth book of poems, YOU, is forthcoming from Coffee House Press in 2024.

Firelei Báez (b. 1981, Dominican Republic) casts diasporic histories into an imaginative realm, re-working visual references drawn from the past to explore new possibilities for the future. With a goal to reclaim power, Báez overlays figuration, symbolic imagery, and abstract gesture onto large-scale reproductions of found maps and documents.

She populates these historically-loaded representations of space with change-making creatures—whose hybrid forms incorporate folkloric and literary references, textile pattern, plantlife, and wide-ranging emblems of healing and resistance—to present fictional alternative universes. She received an M.F.A. from Hunter College, a B.F.A. from the Cooper Union's School of Art, and studied at the Skowhegan School of Painting and Sculpture. In 2020, Báez is shortlisted for Artes Mundi 9, and will be the subject of a solo presentation at the ICA Watershed, Boston, MA this summer. In 2019, the artist had solo exhibitions at the Mennello Museum of Art, Orlando, FL, the Witte de With Center for Contemporary Art, Rotterdam, the Netherlands, and the Modern Window at the Museum of Modern Art, New York. Her major 2015 solo exhibition Bloodlines was organized by the Pérez Art Museum Miami and travelled to the Andy Warhol Museum in Pittsburgh.

Amy Elizabeth Bishop works as a literary agent at Dystel, Goderich & Bourret. Her poetry has or will appear in *Gandy Dancer, The Susquehanna Review, Dialogist,* and *H_NGM_N.* She lives in Queens and you can find her on Twitter at @amylizbishop or on Instagram at @aeb.books.

Nicole Callihan's most recent book is *This Strange Garment,* published by Terrapin Books in March 2023. Her other books include *SuperLoop* and the poetry chapbooks: *The Deeply Flawed Human, Downtown,* and ELSEWHERE (with Zoë Ryder White), as well as a novella, *The Couples.* Her work has appeared in *Kenyon Review, Colorado Review, Conduit, The American Poetry Review,* and as a Poem-a-Day selection from the Academy of American Poets. Find out more at www.nicolecallihan.com.

Amy Sara Carroll's books include *SECESSION; FANNIE + FREDDIE/*

The Sentimentality of Post-9/11 Pornography, and REMEX: *Toward an Art History of the NAFTA Era*. Since 2008, she has been a member of Electronic Disturbance Theater 2.0, coproducing the Transborder Immigrant Tool. She coauthored *[({ })] The Desert Survival Series/La serie de sobrevivencia del desierto* which was published under a Creative Commons license and widely redistributed. Fall 2022, Mexico City's Centro de Cultura Digital included her NFT collection *¡NIFTY! [an intimate oral history/una historia oral íntima]* as a chapbook in the exhibition catalog for *Cuánto tiempo lleva todo esto derramándose sin desbordarse*. Previously she taught at The New School in New York City, currently she's an Associate Professor of Literature and Writing at the University of California, San Diego.

Born in Seoul, South Korea, poet and translator **Don Mee Choi** is the author of *The Morning News Is Exciting* (2010), *Petite Manifesto* (2014), *Hardly War* (2016), and *DMZ Colony* (2020), which won the National Book Award. She has translated many poems from Korean to English, including Kim Hyesoon's books *Mommy Must Be a Fountain of Feathers* (2008); *All the Garbage of the World, Unite!* (2011); *Sorrowtoothpaste Mirrorcream* (2014), a finalist for a PEN Poetry in Translation Award; and *I'm OK, I'm Pig!* (2014). Choi's translations and poetry have appeared in the Massachusetts Review, Trout, the Ampersand Review, Modern Poetry in Translation, and elsewhere. Choi is a winner of the Whiting Award and of the Lucien Stryk Asian Translation Prize. She is also the recipient of a MacArthur Fellowship and a Guggenheim Fellowship. Choi lives in Seattle.

Lucas de Lima is a Brazilian-born poet, artist, scholar, and educator. They are the author of *Wet Land* (Action Books 2014) and *Tropical Sacrifice* (Birds LLC 2022) as well as multiple chapbooks. A recipient of grants and fellowships from the Charlotte W. Newcombe Foundation, the Social Sciences and Humanities Research Council of Canada, and the Canada Council for the Arts, they hold a PhD from the University of Pennsylvania. de Lima lives in New York City and teaches at Mount Holyoke College.

Carina del Valle Schorske is a poet, essayist, and Spanish language translator at large in New York City. Her work has appeared at the *Los Angeles Review of Books, The New Yorker online, Lit Hub, The Point, The New York Times Magazine, The Offing, The Awl,* and elsewhere. She recently won Gulf Coast's 2016 Prize for her translations of the Puerto Rican poet Marigloria Palma. She is the happy recipient of fellowships from CantoMundo, the MacDowell Colony, Bread Loaf, and Columbia University, where she is a doctoral candidate in Comparative Literature. Find her @fluentmundo on Twitter.

A writer and sound artist, **LaTasha N. Nevada Diggs** is the author of *Village* (Coffee House Press 2023) and *TwERK* (Belladonna, 2013). Diggs has presented and performed at California Institute of the Arts, El Museo del Barrio, The Museum of Modern Art, and Walker Art Center and at festivals including: Explore the North Festival, Leeuwarden, Netherlands; Hekayeh Festival, Abu Dhabi; International Poetry Festival of Copenhagen; Ocean Space, Venice; International Poetry Festival of Romania; Question of Will, Slovakia; Poesiefestival, Berlin; and the 2015 Venice Biennale. As an independent curator, artistic director, and producer, Diggs has presented events for BAMCafé, Black Rock Coalition, El Museo del Barrio, La Casita, Lincoln Center Out of Doors, and the David Rubenstein Atrium. LaTasha, with writer Greg Tate, co-founded Coon Bidness, YoYo & SO4 magazine. Diggs has received a 2020 C.D. Wright Award for Poetry from the Foundation of Contemporary Art, a 2016 Whiting Award and a 2015 National Endowment for the Arts Literature Fellowship, as well as grants and fellowships from the Howard Foundation, Cave Canem, Creative Capital, New York Foundation for the Arts, and the U.S.-Japan Friendship Commission, among others. She teaches at Brooklyn and Barnard College.

The Ferrante Project: A collective of 16 women writers of color experimenting with freedom, anti-fame, and anonymity. Contributors include: Cathy Linh Che, Angie Cruz, Natalie Díaz, Ru Freeman, Sarah Gambito Cristina García, Jamey Hatley, Dawn Lundy Martin, Ayana Mathis, Vi khi nao, Aimee Nezhukumatathil, Deborah Paredez, Khadijah Queen, Emily Raboteau, Paisley Rekdal, and Lyrae Van Clief-Stefanon.

Lorgia García-Peña is a Professor of Latinx Studies at Tufts University, the co-founder of Freedom University Georgia, and the author of three books: *Translating Blackness* (2022), *Community as Rebellion* (2022) and *The Borders of Dominicanidad* (Duke 2016). She is the co-editor of the Texas University Press series, *Latinx: the Future is now and the co-director of Archives of Justice*. She writes and teaches in English and Spanish about the intersections of blackness, colonialism and migration, centering Black Latinx lives.

Daisy Hernández is the author of *The Kissing Bug: A True Story of a Family, an Insect, and a Nation's Neglect of a Deadly Disease*, which won the 2022 PEN /Jean Stein Book Award and was selected as an inaugural title for the National Book Foundation's Science + Literature Program. She is also the author of the award-winning memoir *A Cup of Water Under My Bed* and coeditor of *Colonize This! Young Women of Color on Today's Feminism*. She is an Associate Professor at Northwestern University.

Kim Hyesoon is one of the most prominent contemporary poets of South Korea. She lives in Seoul and teaches creative writing at the Seoul Institute of the Arts. Kim's poetry in translation includes *Mommy Must Be a Fountain of Feathers* (Action Books, 2008), *All the Garbage of the World, Unite!* (Action Books, 2011), *Sorrowtoothpaste Mirrorcream* (Action Books, 2014), *I'm OK, I'm Pig!* (Bloodaxe Books, 2014), and *Poor Love Machine* (Action Books, 2016).

Lucia Hierro (b. 1987) is a Dominican American conceptual artist born and raised in New York City, Washington Heights/Inwood, and currently based in the South Bronx. Lucia's practice, which includes sculpture, digital media and installation, confronts twenty-first century capitalism through an intersectional lens. Hierro's work has been exhibited at venues including the Bronx Museum of the Arts, the Museum of the African Diaspora (MoAD) in San Francisco, Jeffrey Deitch Gallery (Los Angeles), Elizabeth Dee Gallery (New York), Latchkey Projects (New York), Primary Projects (Miami), Sean Horton Presents (Dallas), and Casa Quien in the Dominican Republic. Her works reside in the collections of the Pérez Art Museum Miami, the JP Morgan & Chase Collection, Progressive Art Collection, and the Rennie collection in Vancouver, among others, as well as in the collection of the Guggenheim Museum, New York.

Marlin M. Jenkins was born and raised in Detroit. The author of the poetry chapbook *Capable Monsters* (Bull City Press, 2020) and a graduate of University of Michigan's MFA program, their work has found homes with *Indiana Review, Iowa Review, TriQuarterly, Waxwing, Kenyon Review Online*, and *The Rumpus*. They currently live and teach in Minnesota.

Joe Jiménez is the author of *The Possibilities of Mud* (Korima 2014) and Bloodline (Arte Público 2016). Jiménez is the recipient of the 2016 Letras Latinas/Red Hen Press Poetry Prize. Jimenez's essays and poems have appeared in *The Adroit Journal, Iron Horse, RHINO, Bat City,* and *Waxwing,* and on the PBS NewsHour and Lambda Literary sites. Jimenez was recently awarded a Lucas Artists Literary Artists Fellowship from 2017-2020. He lives in San Antonio, Texas, and is a member of the Macondo Writing Workshops. For more information, visit joejimenez.net

Rosamond S. King is a creative and critical writer, performer, and artist whose work is deeply informed by her cultures and communities, by history, and by a sense of play. Her poetry has appeared in more than two dozen journals and anthologies, and her manuscript Rock|*Salt*|*Stone* is forthcoming from Nightboat Books. King has performed in Africa, the Caribbean, Europe, and throughout North America. She is an Associate Professor at Brooklyn College and author of the award-winning scholarly book *Island Bodies: Transgressive Sexualities in the Caribbean Imagination.* Her goal is to make people feel, wonder, and think, in that order.

Shayla Lawz was raised in Jersey City, NJ. She is a graduate of Rutgers University, where she studied English and Philosophy. She writes poetry, fiction, and non-fiction that often deals with childhood, color, and the body. Currently, she lives in Providence, RI where she is an MFA candidate in Literary Arts at Brown University. Her work has been featured in Winter Tangerine.

Karen An-hwei Lee is the author of *Duress* (Cascade 2022), *Rose is a Verb: Neo-Georgics* (Slant 2021), *Phyla of Joy* (Tupelo 2012), *Ardor* (Tupelo 2008) and *In Medias Res* (Sarabande 2004), winner of the Norma Farber First Book Award. Her book of literary criticism,

Anglophone Literatures in the Asian Diaspora: Literary Transnationalism and Translingual Migrations, was selected for the Cambria Sinophone World Series (2013). She serves as provost and a professor of English at Wheaton College.

Marie Myung-Ok Lee is a founder of the Asian American Writers' Workshop and teaches creative writing at Columbia, where she is Writer in Residence. She was a winner of the War & Peace faculty initiative grant for *The Evening Hero* and has written about the Korean War for *Gen Magazine, Salon,* and most recently for Ibram X. Kendi's journal, *The Emancipator*. One of a handful of American journalists who have been granted a visa to North Korea since the Korean War, Lee was also the first Fulbright Scholar to Korea in creative writing and has received many honors for her work, including an O. Henry honorable mention, the Best Book Award from the Friends of American Writers, and a New York Foundation for the Arts fiction fellowship. Her stories and essays have been published in *The Atlantic, The New York Times, Slate, Salon, Guernica, The Paris Review, The Nation,* and *The Guardian,* among others. She has appeared on CNN's The Situation Room with Wolf Blitzer talking about diplomacy in North Korea and on Dr. Sanjay Gupta's program Weed, discussing being the first parent to use cannabis for her son with autism. She is a staff writer for *The Millions* and a board member of the National Book Critics Circle.

Carley Moore is the author of *Panpocalypse, The Not Wives, 16 Pills,* and *The Stalker Chronicles*. Carley has two poetry collections, *My First Queer Year* and *Heartless* forthcoming from Tinderbox Editions and Indolent Press. She's a Clinical Professor of Writing and Creative Production at New York University and she lives in Brooklyn. Follow her on Instagram @fragmentedsky or find her blogging on Substack.

Courtney Desiree Morris is an assistant professor of African American and Women's studies at Pennsylvania State University and studies Black women's social movements in Latin America and the Caribbean. She received her PhD in Anthropology at the University of Texas at Austin. Her research focuses on Afro-Nicaraguan women's political activism since the Sandinista Revolution and she is currently completing a book on this research. She is a recipient of the Ford Foundation Pre-Doctoral Diversity Fellowship and a Fulbright.

Marigloria Palma was born Gloria María Pagán y Ferrer in 1915. Records differ regarding her birthplace—either Loiza or Canovanas, Puerto Rico—but she was raised by her working-class single mother before leaving school to work first as a maid and later as an assistant to a photographer in San Juan, the island's capital. In 1942, she was the second woman (after Julia de Burgos) to receive the island's premier poetry prize from the Institute of Culture. She cultivated a wide-ranging creative practice—folklore, children's literature, theater, poetry, fiction, drawing, and painting—over her fifty year career.

Christina Olivares is the author of *No Map of the Earth Includes Stars*, winner of the 2014 Marsh Hawk Press Book Prize, of the chaplet *Interrupt*, published by Belladonna* Series, and of DSM/Partial Manual, winner of the 2014 Vinyl 45 Chapbook Competition . She is the recipient of a 2015-2016 LMCC Workspace Residency, two Jerome Foundation Travel and Study Grants (2010 and 2014), a 2008 Teachers and Writers Fellowship, and has twice been nominated for a Pushcart Prize.

Norma Liliana Valdez is the author of the chapbook *Preparing the Body* (YesYes Books, 2019). A member of the Macondo Writers Workshop and a CantoMundo fellow, her poems appear in *Waxwing Literary*

Journal, The Los Angeles Review, PANK Magazine, and Tinderbox Poetry Journal, among others. She has been awarded residencies and fellowships from Hedgebrook, Under the Volcano International, and Community of Writers.

Cecilia Vicuña is a poet, visual artist and filmmaker born in Santiago de Chile. The author of twenty two books of poetry, she exhibits and performs internationally. In Chile, she founded the legendary Tribu Noin 1967, a group that created anonymous poetic actions throughout the city. In 1974, exiled in London, she co-founded Artists for Democracy.

Acknowledgments

"Reparations" by Rosamond S. King was first published in Rock|Salt|Stone (2017, Nightboat Books).

We believe "Este Momento Mío" by Marigloria Palma was first published previously elsewhere, but we unfortunately are not able to find records; all of her books are sadly out-of-print.

Rosa Alcalá's translations of Cecilia Vicuna's poems are from Vicuna's first book, Sabor a Mí (1973), and were re-published after appearing in Aster(ix) in Cecilia Vicuña: New & Selected Poems (Kelsey Street Press, 2018).

"The Patient Records" by The Ferrante Project was also featured/published in 2020 in The Point Mag.

"The Patient Records" and "Death of a Family" are from The Ferrante Project: The freedom of anonymity, brings together sixteen women writers of color to anonymously contribute new works as an investment in possibility and the possibility for failure. To get to something that we might call "art," to give women writers a unique venue to do something that they would not normally do in writing, to open something up in their own creative processes. Although most of us felt prompted by a need to step out of prescribed roles as mothers, professors, organizers, and spokeswomen to write liberated from expectations and duty, common themes in the work for this project include physical decline, menopause, mental health, resentment, and rage against patriarchy. See the Fall 2020 Aster(ix) issue, *The Ferrante Project*, for more information.

"A Lullaby" by Kim Hyesoowas originally published by Action Books.

If you enjoyed this issue of *Aster(ix)*
and want to share or see more of our work,
please visit www.asterixjournal.com
or scan the QR code below:

@asterixjournal